I *almost* Love You, Eddie Clegg

AUDRA SUPPLEE

PEACHTREE

CP
JR

Published by
PEACHTREE PUBLISHERS, LTD.
1700 Chattahoochee Avenue
Atlanta, Georgia 30318-2112

www.peachtree-online.com

Cover design by Loraine M. Joyner
Book design by Melanie M. McMahon

Manufactured in the United States of America
10 9 8 7 6 5 4 3 2 1
First Edition

ISBN 1-56145-308-0

Library of Congress Cataloging-in-Publication Data

Supplee, Audra.
  I almost love you, Eddie Clegg / written by Audra Supplee.-- 1st ed.
     p. cm.
Summary: A thirteen-year-old and her recovering alcoholic stepfather
forge an awkward father-daughter relationship as she embarks on a quest
for popularity and romance and he struggles with the loss of his job.
  ISBN 1-56145-308-0
  [1. Stepfathers--Fiction. 2. Alcoholism--Fiction. 3. Fathers and
daughters--Fiction. 4. Unemployment--Fiction.] I. Title.
  PZ7.S96515 Iae 2004
  [Fic]--dc22
                                2003018745

For Mom and the Fabulous Four:
Brian, Sharon, Joel, and Eric

Chapter One

The first Wednesday in August is always Back-to-School Shopping Day at my house. And shopping with my mom is worse than getting your teeth drilled without Novocaine.

Mom means well, but she always ruins everything by following me into every store. Then she tries to talk me out of buying the clothes I really want. Her favorite line is, "Are you sure you want that shade of orange, Asa Marie?"

Just because there's a hint of red in my hair, she thinks I'll clash. But *she's* the one with the bright red hair and the clashing problem.

I had no appetite at breakfast. On shopping days nothing tastes good. Not even chocolate frosted Pop-Tarts. That's why I made myself the king of bland cereals, cream of wheat. My stomach already felt miserable so it didn't care if it got food with no flavor.

My stepdad sat at the end of the table. He ate Lucky Charms. My insides knew better than to feel jealous that he got the fun-tasting cereal.

Mom bustled into the dining area, kicking up a cloud of sugary perfume.

"Change of plans, everyone," she said. She plopped into her seat across from my stepdad and smiled at him. "Custody emergency, honey. Looks like Rodger needs me at the office after all."

An eager pulse whooshed through my ears. Maybe Mom would let me shop with my friends this year. After all, I was thirteen. This was my last year of middle school. Shouldn't that earn me a few maturity points?

Mom took an apple out of the fruit basket in the middle of the table. "Eddie, you're off today," she said casually. "Why don't you take Asa shopping?"

He choked on a mini marshmallow. "Who, me?" he rasped.

Even though we've been a family for almost six years, Eddie and I don't do many things together. Whenever we do, one of us usually gets mad. Then we don't speak to each other for days.

"Can't I just shop on my own?" I asked. It was Eddie's turn to stop speaking. I didn't feel like getting snubbed today.

Mom ignored me. "Make sure she doesn't buy anything trashy. I don't want her going to school looking like a tramp."

Trashy? Tramp? Where did she get these ideas? Tramps wore short leather skirts and skin-tight spandex pants. Mom knew I was a jeans and sweater person. Did she think I'd had a personality change overnight?

I wanted to argue, but no one would have heard me. Eddie was making too much noise, hacking and thumping his chest. Mom leaped up and gave him a glass of water. She rubbed his back while he drained the glass in two swallows.

"Maybe you should reschedule, Lynnie," he said, puffing for breath. "I don't know what tramps wear these days. I might not know if she's—"

"Edward," Mom said, flashing her green eyes at him.

2

"You're going." She set her jaw in the I-mean-business position. Nobody argued with that jaw, not even Eddie.

He rubbed his cheek a couple times.

"And don't forget underwear," Mom said on her way out the door.

"Mom!" I squealed.

Eddie's eyes bugged out. *What?*

After she left us, the house turned dead quiet. I saw the wrinkles coming out in Eddie's forehead. It looked like he dreaded this shopping trip as much as I did.

"Um," I began. "Maybe you could—" I hesitated when his long-lashed eyes focused on me. I peered into my cream of wheat. "—just drop me off?" I crossed my fingers under the table.

"Your mother wants me to supervise," Eddie said. "Although I don't know where she gets the idea I could possibly know anything about…"

I looked up. He glanced away.

"…girl shopping," he mumbled.

"That's why you should let me do it," I said. "I know all about girl shopping. Plus, I promise not to buy any tramp clothes."

Eddie tapped his chin and gazed at the ceiling. Finally he looked at me. "Here's how we'll do it," he said. "We'll go to the mall and separate. You get your non-tramp clothes on your own, but I'll be nearby. Check in with me so I'll know you're buying the right things. Then we can have pizza at Rollo's for lunch."

"Yes!" I squealed. I almost hugged him. Instead, I jumped up and toasted myself a chocolate frosted Pop-Tart. It tasted delicious.

At the mall Eddie handed over the credit card. "You'll know where to find me if you need me," he said.

I nodded. Eddie loved music shops. That's because he was a music-head. He taught music at Ram's Head College. He was also the conductor for our community orchestra. I left him to his music quest and scurried to my first store.

Who would have guessed how easy it was to shop alone! Nobody told me to try stuff on to be sure it fit. Nobody made faces at the patterns on the shirts I liked. Nobody complained about the prices. Since I was using a credit card, it was almost like it was free anyway. But to keep Mom happy I shopped at the cheaper stores and made sure I bought clothes on sale.

I was practically done when I saw two popular girls from school breeze into The Sophisticated Miss. That shop is so expensive Mom won't even let me breathe the air in there. The girls didn't notice me, but I didn't mind. They'd notice me in September when I turned popular too. I'd gotten the idea over the summer to become popular because this was my last year at Wollerton Middle School. Why not go out with a bang?

The quickest way to popularity was to join The Fad. Every fall at Wollerton the popular girls started a new one. Two years ago they tied colored ribbons to their left wrists. I didn't feel like joining that year. The ribbons reminded me of when parents tie balloon strings to their little kids' wrists so they won't fly away. The balloons, I mean. Not the little kids.

Here's the thing about fads: Anybody can join. Even people at the outer fringe of the popularity circle (which is where I was, unfortunately). All you had to do was figure out what the fad was. I don't know why nobody else on the outer fringe had thought of doing it. My latest scheme had been to take a baby-sitting job at the house next door to Jennifer Terrell. She was the girl in charge of fads.

Joining wouldn't be easy, though. The clique changed the rules so fast you could turn unpopular again in the blink of an eye if you didn't keep up. During "ribbon" year Angela Rush fell out of the loop. All because she wouldn't let a girl we call Snooty Ella copy off her paper during a math quiz. Somebody—probably Snooty Ella—told Angela that the next day's ribbon colors were green and gold. Everybody else wore pink and maroon. Angela spent hours crying in the girls' room because everybody started calling her OT. That's a shortened version of OTWCW, which means "Out of Touch With the Cool World." Everybody knows you can't be popular if you're OT.

Last year the girls wore neckties as belts. I almost decided to try out for popularity then, but I couldn't join that fad. Eddie owned the wrong kind of ties. Mom wouldn't even let me buy my own ties at the Salvation Army. She said I should want to be my own woman. That was her polite way of asking the age-old question: if all your friends jumped off a cliff, would you want to jump too? Mom doesn't get it sometimes. It's a lot easier to be your own woman when you're thirty-five, like she is. Especially when you follow your own drumbeat, which my mom does—literally. She practices the drums all the time in our basement when she isn't studying to be a paralegal.

If I wanted my last year at middle school to be huge, I had to join this year's fad. I'd heard a rumor that the fad might be special shoes. There was also talk around the pool at the Y about braiding different colored feathers in your hair. I hoped that wasn't it. My hair was too short for braids.

So far, my job next door to Jennifer Terrell had been a

bust. Jennifer went away to equestrian camp the day before my baby-sitting job started. My only consolation was that she had to come home eventually. And when she did, I'd have to be ready.

But for now, I needed underwear. On the way to Sears, I spotted Eddie at the back of The Musical Box, where you can sample new CDs. I decided to duck inside for a second to leave my shopping bag with him. When I bought underwear, I liked to travel light.

A pair of black headphones covered Eddie's ears. His eyes were closed. His right hand swayed a little, like he was conducting. With him, it was almost a reflex. I just wished he wouldn't do it in public without any actual musicians playing. I glanced around to make sure nobody I knew was in the store. Then I moved closer to him.

Mom apparently hasn't noticed, but after six years I still don't have a name for her second husband. I couldn't call him Eddie to his face. That might sound disrespectful. And Mr. Clegg seemed way too formal. But even though he's my stepfather, I wouldn't dare call him Dad. He might not like it. And I'm not sure if I'd want to call him Dad, anyway. If we're in a crowd and I need to talk to him, I either tap his arm or wait till he looks at me. This time I touched his shoulder to get his attention.

Eddie's eyes snapped open. He blinked a few times as he came out of his trance.

"Hey, Ace," he said. He pushed the headphones back so they hung around his neck. Violin music whispered from the little speakers. "What've ya got?"

I opened my bag. I pulled out my new sweaters and pants one at a time.

Chapter One

Eddie stared hard at a pair of black jeans. He wanted to know if they were tramp tight. I promised they weren't and showed him the rest of my non-tramp selections.

"Lynnie should approve," he said with a dimpled smile.

"Then let's tell her I can shop alone from now on," I said.

"No!" Eddie's smile turned into wide-eyed panic. "Let her think I helped, okay?"

I stared at the tangle of pant legs and sweaters in my shopping bag. I'd bought them on my own. Why couldn't we say I did?

"Just this once," he begged. "Please, Ace?"

I slowly raised my head. If I did him this one favor maybe we'd break the "no speaking" curse. I nodded.

Eddie grinned and thumped me under the chin. He went back to listening to violin music through the headphones. I set my bag by his feet and took off again.

It was time for the super-private part of my shopping: buying underwear. Now I was really glad Eddie wasn't tagging along. Thanks to the baggy shirts I always wore, not even Mom knew my bra size had jumped from zero to 34A over the summer. I know women are supposed to feel proud of their breasts, but I wasn't ready to show them off yet.

I ducked into Sears and slipped between the clothes racks to the intimate apparel department. Four sports bras and two packs of boy shorts later, I let myself breathe again. On the ride down the escalator I spotted Jennifer Terrell. *Aha!* I thought, *equestrian camp must be over for the summer.* Jennifer was sitting alone. She was almost hidden by the leaves of a tall tree, but I recognized her shiny black ponytail and poised posture. She's gorgeous and popular. She's also rich. Rich enough to go to private school, but she didn't. I heard a rumor that her dad had insisted that she go to public school since it was good enough for him when he was a kid.

My heart thumped. This was my chance to walk straight up to Jennifer Terrell and ask her about this year's fad.

Secret confession: I have never actually spoken to Jennifer. Not even to say, "Hey, you dropped this." I needed a creative entrance. Like…maybe a rolling orange. If I had a bag of oranges and one dropped and rolled past her, I'd have to chase it. Then, as I picked it up, I could turn to Jennifer and say, "Don't you hate it when oranges do that?"

Do malls even have fruit stands? I snapped my head left to right. My eyes zeroed in on the shop closest to me, The Drug Emporium. I went inside and stepped back out in about a minute. A can of Orange Crush sweated in my hand. True, it wasn't the fruit, but it was the right color. And it rolled.

I edged toward Jennifer's bench. Using the splashing of the nearby water fountain as cover, I laid the can on its side and kicked it. The can didn't roll past Jennifer. It turned and bounced against her shiny black shoes.

Jennifer looked up. That's when I noticed she was crying. The most popular girl in school with tears rolling down her cheeks! Now that was something you didn't see every day. It made her almost seem like a regular person. Like somebody who needed a friend.

I walked over very casually. "You okay?" I asked.

She sniffled and nodded. "Allergies." She picked up my Orange Crush and handed it to me. "Yours?" she asked. Then she looked at me again. "I know you. Asa Philips, right?"

"You do?" I was so surprised I sat down right next to her.

Jennifer looked at me with big, brown eyes. The corners of her lips curled into a little smile. "Remember two years ago when we had trampoline in gym class? You wore a towel around your neck like a cape and kept yelling you were Super Something."

"Super Amazing Towel Girl,'" I said. That was one of the few times I'd tried to be funny on purpose. I even came close to turning popular that day. But that was sixth grade. Eighth graders didn't get popular that way.

"You were sure gutsy to look stupid like that."

I shrugged and looked away, embarrassed. "Or just stupid."

We laughed together. A second later our smiles faded. I set down my soda can. "So, uh, why are you sad?"

Jennifer sighed. "My parents are on their way to France right now and I'm stuck here in boring Pennsylvania with my grandmother and our housekeeper."

"If my parents left me alone with my grandma," I said, "we'd have pizza every night."

Jennifer sighed again. "Only Super Amazing Towel Girl would find a bright side like that."

At first I wasn't sure if that was a compliment or an insult. I didn't have to wonder too long. Jennifer turned to me and said, "Want to get pizza at Rollo's?"

I tried to sound bored when I said, "Sure," but on the inside I was celebrating all over the place. Jennifer Terrell, the most popular girl at Wollerton Middle School, had just invited me to lunch at Rollo's! This was bigger than fireworks at Disney World. This was even bigger than the time I rode the elephant at the Renaissance Faire.

Okay, technically, I was supposed to meet Eddie at Rollo's, but he was probably still conducting to himself. At least I hoped he was. I wanted to eat lunch with Jennifer.

At the counter Jennifer ordered a large pepperoni and drinks. I offered to pay for my share, but she just waved me off. We carried our paper cups, fizzing with cola, to a table. We had a perfect view of another fountain outside in the mall.

If I wanted to learn about The Fad, now was my chance. I took a swallow of cola for courage. "So, it's our last year at Wollerton."

"Yeah," Jennifer said. "Things sure will be different."

My stomach and my heart bumped into each other. It was time to ask the big question. But before I could open my mouth, Jennifer ducked under the table.

"Act natural," she said in a nervous voice.

The only natural thing I could do was frown in confusion and peer under the table at her. "What are you doing?" I asked.

"Don't look at me!" she said in a desperate whisper. "I just saw Lacy and Mindy. They can't catch us talking. No offense."

I shrugged, willing to play along. For now. Once I got popular this wouldn't be a problem. I watched two girls in short skirts and designer handbags whisk by. "They're gone," I murmured out of the corner of my mouth. I felt like a double agent.

Jennifer poked her head over the table. She let out a sigh and sat up. "Sorry about that. If you were part of the group..."

"Like somebody who knew the fad?" I said in a casual, hint-hint voice.

"That's it!" Jennifer clutched my arm. "You should join! This one's perfect for you. It's—" Then she suddenly cut herself off and looked straight ahead. "Hey, who's that?"

I looked up. Eddie was standing in front of the fountain,

facing us. I choked on air. Fortunately, he looked younger than his actual age. Doubly fortunately for me, he didn't call my name. He didn't make any noise at all. He just stood there and acted like a mime, pretending to be stuck in a box. Jennifer had no way of knowing that was my shopping bag resting at his feet. If he ruined my lunch with the most popular girl in school, I'd never speak to him again. Less than an hour ago we were practically bonding. Why did he have to show up now?

"Doesn't he look familiar?" asked Jennifer. "I could swear..." her voice trailed away.

"Never saw him before in my life," I blurted.

"I'm sure I've seen him before," said Jennifer. "On TV, I think."

"I'm more of a reader, myself," I lied.

"Ages ago, on cable," Jennifer said. She snapped her fingers. "I know! The Looney Clooney Clown show! He was Looney's sidekick, Mr. Music! The mute musician. He couldn't talk. He just played musical instruments. Didn't you ever see it when you were a little kid?"

I let out a sigh. "Maybe once or twice."

I personally was not a fan. Years ago Mom had found the show by accident when I was sick. She was flipping through the channels on the remote and stopped when she saw this skinny guy, dressed in a white suit with piano keys and black music notes all over it. Mom had let out a whoop. "I can't believe it, that's Eddie Clegg!"

Talk about a small world. She knew the weird skinny guy from college.

Jennifer sprang from her seat and ran into the mall. I dashed after her.

"You used to be Mr. Music, didn't you?" Jennifer said to Eddie.

He just nodded. Then he gave me a suspicious stare like I put her up to this.

Jennifer beamed at him. "When I was little, my parents wanted me to play the violin. I hated it. Then I saw you play one on the Looney Clooney Show. You made it sound like magic."

Eddie smiled back. "Did that encourage you to practice?"

Jennifer gaped at him. "You *can* talk! He can talk!" she said to me. "I didn't think he—" She turned back to Eddie. "I mean, I didn't think you could talk."

"The character couldn't talk," Eddie told her. "But I'm—"

"—just a regular guy now," I jumped in before he could say he was my stepdad.

Eddie gave me a baffled frown.

"You were so good on that show!" said Jennifer. "I loved it the time you made a guitar out of rubber bands and a shoe box."

"Did you take up the guitar?" Eddie asked, sounding pleased.

She giggled. "Nope, I took up the shoe box and rubber bands. I'm Jennifer, by the way. This is Asa."

"Asa," he said, shaking my hand. "Have we met?"

"Don't think so," I said. I cringed inside, afraid he might not keep playing along.

Eddie turned from me and smiled at Jennifer. "It was nice meeting you. I was just on the way to my car. I'll be waiting there exactly five minutes." He held his watch under my nose and tapped the place where the minute hand would be in five minutes. "I sure hope the person I gave a ride to meets me then. I'd hate to have to come back."

"We understand. Prior commitments," I said. "See ya."

He pivoted on his heel and toted my school clothes out the exit.

"He's still kind of cute," Jennifer whispered on the way back to our table.

"If you like old guys. He's thirty-three."

"How do you know him?"

"Uh, a friend of the family."

I wanted to talk about fads. Jennifer talked about Mr. Music. She told me when she was a kid her dad spent so much time away on business that she sort of adopted Mr. Music as her imaginary dad. She loved it when Mr. Music drummed on his top hat. And wasn't it funny every time he played the trombone and the slide kept getting caught in his suspenders?

Yeah, I thought. *Real funny.*

The seconds zipped by on my own watch. Pretty soon my time would be up. If Eddie came back to get me, would Jennifer like it that her big hero was my stepdad or would she be mad that I'd lied? Just in case she hated liars, there was only one solution: I had to vanish. Fast.

The pizza guy called out her number. As soon as Jennifer headed toward the counter, I ran out of Rollo's. Stupid Eddie and his stupid time limits. Jennifer would never speak to me again.

I dove into Eddie's back seat just in case Jennifer was looking out the window at the parking lot. "Go, go!" I squealed.

Eddie grunted and started the car. About a mile from the mall, he pulled over to the side of the road.

"Get up here. I'm not the chauffeur."

Never argue with a grouchy voice. I clicked into the shoulder strap in the front seat. Eddie pulled back onto the road. A tense silence bounced between us. He broke it first. "Would you mind explaining why you can't recognize me in public?"

My mom's second husband had a good profile. His nose was straight with the right amount of roundness at the tip. It didn't turn up like a pixie nose the way mine did.

"I'm allowed to recognize *you*," I told him. " I just can't recognize Mr. Music."

I knew that was the wrong answer by the way Eddie's jaw tightened. He acted like I was the bad guy when he was the one who'd ruined everything by being the ex–Mr. Music in the first place. Neither of us spoke again until I reached for the radio knob.

"Leave it," he said. "I'm composing."

He did that sometimes, wrote music in his head. But I didn't think that's what he was doing this time. He wasn't speaking to me, that's what he was doing. I knew at breakfast it would be his turn today. What Eddie didn't realize was, I wasn't speaking to him either.

Back home he stomped down to the basement and played depressing jazz music on his sax. I didn't need any music to remind me how bad things were. I had just blown my one chance to become popular.

Chapter Two

After I ran out on the most popular girl in school I didn't dare face her the very next day at my baby-sitting job. I needed at least a week to think up a good excuse. Alien abduction? Lost in an alternate universe? Were popular kids gullible?

I tried to tell Mom I had cramps and couldn't baby-sit. She said I'd feel better if I kept active and made me ride my bike to work anyway. On the plus side, Jennifer lived in a development with huge yards. It was possible to play outside and not be seen.

I found the perfect hiding place. I invited my baby-sitting client, Abby, to a tea party behind her parents' gazebo. Nobody would see us there. But Abby didn't want to drink fake tea or to hide behind gazebos. She wanted to make mud pies. I had to blame myself for that. I was the one who had taught her how much fun it was to play in dirt. Almost every day we made mud pies in the corner of her parents' vegetable garden. While Jennifer was at equestrian camp I didn't care that Abby's garden had a perfect view of Jennifer's hilly lawn and Jennifer's whitewashed post-and-rail fence. But I cared now. If Jennifer stepped outside and looked down her hill, she'd see us for sure. She'd stomp down that hill. Then she'd scream, "Why did you leave me alone in Rollo's with a whole pepperoni pizza?"

What could I say? I had developed a sudden allergy to mozzarella?

"I could really go for a tea party right about now," I told Abby.

She folded her little arms. "I could really go for a mud pie."

Since it was Abby's turn to be the boss, I had to follow her to the garden. I poured the water onto the dirt. Every few seconds I checked over my shoulder to see if Jennifer was coming to yell at me. I almost gave myself whiplash. Five minutes passed. Jennifer didn't appear. Maybe she'd gone back to riding camp.

Wispy clouds puffed across a pale blue sky. It was a good day to squish in the mud with a four-year-old kid. Finally, I started to relax. Then a perfect shadow rolled over the rusty-colored puddle Abby had made.

"Well, well," said a sarcastic voice from above. "Look who's here."

My head snapped up. Jennifer was leaning against her side of the white fence.

I pushed my toy shovel into Abby's dimpled hand and leaped up. The plan was to get away from the dirt so I'd at least look dignified. But half the garden was still attached to my knees.

"Hi. Uh, sorry about yesterday." My mind raced for a perfect excuse. I felt like the Grinch when Cindy-Lou Who caught him stealing her Christmas tree. And just like the Grinch, I came up with a clever lie almost immediately. "Remember Lacy and Heather?" I said.

"Lacy and Mindy," she corrected. Suddenly Jennifer's eyes widened. "You mean they came back? They didn't see you, did they?"

"Nope," I said. I knew the rules. Other popular kids weren't allowed to see me with Jennifer until I was part of The Fad.

Jennifer let out a big sigh. "You saved us both a lot of hassle."

"That's why I left," I lied, nodding.

"I know my friends can be a little, you know…"

"Snooty?" I filled in.

Jennifer raised one eyebrow. "I was going to say narrow-minded. If they got to know you I'm sure they'd like you. Except for running out on me, you did make me feel better yesterday. You just have a way of doing that kind of stuff, you know? Like Super Amazing Towel Girl."

I smiled modestly.

"And I still have to laugh when I think about the time you got hiccups at chorus practice."

My smile froze. Just remembering that day made my cheeks burn. There we were, two dozen kids in the auditorium, but only one of us had the hiccups. The acoustics were so good everybody heard me. It also sounded like the whole world started laughing at me. No matter how hard I held my breath, I still squeaked and hicked through "Ode to Joy." I wanted to melt into a wad of gum on the floor.

Just then Abby called out, "See this, Asa? I'm making cake now!"

I waved to her. "Good job."

"I think it's great you can play with a little kid like that," said Jennifer. "I'm a terrible baby-sitter. I can't stand sitting in mud."

Not the way she was dressed today, anyway. She wore a pink and white striped top with white shorts. Even her sandals were pink and white.

I wore faded navy gym shorts and my stepdad's Ram's Head College sweatshirt with the sleeves chopped off. In other words…mud clothes.

A gust of warm air blew by. My red-brown hair was too short for the wind to ruffle it much. The breeze pulled strands of shiny black hair out of Jennifer's ponytail. She slid her fingers through the dancing wisps. She closed her eyes and turned her face to the sun.

Just like everything else, her face was perfect. There wasn't a pimple in sight. I wore bangs to hide the little ones that sprouted on my forehead when I wasn't looking. I won't even mention how much all the freckles on my cheeks and nose bug me.

Jennifer opened her eyes again. "The fad's Silhouette Racing Shoes this year," she said suddenly. "Don't tell anybody I told. If you come to school wearing Silhouettes, like the rest of us…" Jennifer shrugged.

If I wore Silhouettes like the rest of them, I'd be popular! I gulped. "So all I need are shoes and I'm in the fad?"

"It's not just the shoes," Jennifer said. "You have to replace the black laces with colored ones. A mixed pair per shoe."

"Oh, right," I said. It reminded me of the ribbon fad from sixth grade.

"On the first day we'll wear brown and orange laces, in honor of fall. The next time we'll wear the school colors."

The secret list! She was giving me the secret list!

Too bad I'd spent all my birthday money on a mini CD player last month. How was I going to pay for all this stuff?

"You'll need at least twelve pairs of laces," Jennifer went on. "Gold and silver are a must, by the way. Ally's Attic sells them."

I knew Ally's Attic. It was a fancy art supply shop that also sold candy. Eddie stopped there for red licorice whips almost every day. Sure, the candy was reasonably priced, but everything else was ridiculous. Once I almost bought a mini pencil sharpener in there until I saw the $8.99 price tag. If Ally's sold laces they probably wouldn't be cheap. That meant I'd have to scrape up enough money to buy laces *and* Silhouette Racing Shoes, whatever those were. I'd check the Internet when I got home.

First, I changed Abby's muddy clothes before her mom came home. Time moves fast when you're rinsing out little kid clothes in the bathroom sink and thinking about fads. When my baby-sitting shift ended, I waved good-bye to Abby and hopped on my bike. Then I zoomed down the hill toward town.

I live in Ram's Head, Pennsylvania. The town got its name from a tavern back in colonial times. It is exactly halfway between Philadelphia and Wilmington, Delaware. Now Ram's Head is a college town. A First National Bank replaced the tavern, but the name stuck. Now our college mascot is a male sheep.

Ram's Head is so small you can go just about anywhere on foot or a bike. Ginger Lane, where I live, is less than three miles from the center of town. My blue ranch house stands between the Weber family's white ranch on the right and old Mr. Murphy's green one on the left.

I rolled into my empty drive. Usually I entered through the garage, but today I'd forgotten my remote. I leaned my bike against a bush and unlocked the front door. TV noises came from the family room. That wasn't right. Nobody was supposed to be home. Mom was at work. Eddie had a community orchestra meeting.

"Hello?" I shouted from the front door. If a burglar was in there, I wanted to know before I stepped all the way inside.

There was no answer. All I heard was hokey horror music coming from the TV. I tiptoed through the living room and dining area and finally relaxed when I spotted Eddie on the couch in the family room. He was hugging a throw pillow and gazing at a black and white movie playing on cable.

"Where's your car?" I asked.

"Garage," he said, his eyes focused on the screen. "Didn't you come in that way?"

"No remote. I used the front door. How come you're home?"

He frowned, still not looking up. "How come *you* are?"

It looked like this was going to be another grumpy conversation day.

A lump of dried mud cracked at my knee and fell on the carpet. Even though Eddie never yells at me (that's Mom's job), I still cringed. I expected him at least to scowl over the mess. But he didn't seem to notice. I knew Mom would, so I scooped up the mud chips. I sprinted to the kitchen sink and rinsed my legs. Then I darted around the snack bar, still dripping, and raced back to the family room.

Eddie didn't glance at the water or me. He was too busy being a zombie, just like the ones he was watching on TV.

I pounced on the magazine rack where we kept old catalogs. Sometimes flipping through a catalog can be quicker than going online. If you can find the catalog, that is. The one I wanted was buried under half a zillion back issues of *Modern Drummer* and *Musician Magazine,* but I found it.

I whipped through the pages. There they were in the sports section: Silhouette Racing Shoes. Seventy-nine ninety-nine on sale.

They were leather high-tops, totally black except for a hologram of a purple lightning bolt on the side. They were awesome. I had to have those shoes, fad or not.

I left Eddie sulking and raced back to my bike. I pedaled to Rodger L. Ridgeway, Esquire's law office in the center of town. Mom worked there part-time as a legal assistant. It was a ten-minute bike ride from my house.

I waved to the receptionist and scampered up the stairs to Mom's office.

"Hey, sweet cakes!" Mom greeted me with a big smile.

Mr. Ridgeway must be in court, I thought. Whenever he was in the office, Mom acted a lot more serious.

Mom pushed her reading glasses up on the top of her head. Two hanks of her red hair sprang out like floppy horns. "Feel like making copies of that property settlement agreement?" She nodded at a short stack of paper in her out basket. "The phone's been nuts today. I haven't even opened the mail."

If I made the copies, maybe Mom would feel generous and help out with the shoes. I carried the papers to the copy machine across from her desk.

Mom flipped down her glasses again and tore open her first letter. A few phone calls came in but she handled them in her usual take-charge way.

The copier hummed and spit out paper. It didn't jam a single time.

"What's up with Eddie?" I asked. "He's home watching old horror movies."

"Oh, no," said Mom, frowning. "I bet the community orchestra lost its funding. He's been worried about that. Did he look depressed?"

I shrugged and copied more pages. Eddie just looked

grouchy to me. But what if the orchestra couldn't keep Eddie on as conductor? That would mean one less paycheck every month. Now *I* felt depressed. How could I ask for Silhouette Racing Shoes if Eddie had just lost his part-time job?

"He loved that orchestra," Mom said absently. "We'll have to cheer him up." She opened another envelope. "I know! Let's buy him some of that red licorice he likes. I think we can still afford a little candy."

I knew we could get Eddie's favorite licorice at just about any grocery store, but I talked Mom into going to Ally's Attic.

After work we put my bike in the trunk of Mom's car and drove to Ally's. It was a block from the college on Main Street. The shop smelled like sugar and scented candles. Mom marched to the counter where the jars of different flavored licorice whips stood. Strawberry was Eddie's favorite. I heard Mom order a dozen of the giant whips.

I wandered between shelves filled with fake flowers and art supplies, looking for shoelaces. Two aisles later I found them. They hung from hooks next to a pile of teddy bears. There were baby shoelaces with pink rattles on them. There were medium-sized laces with pastel colored balloons on them. There were sneaker laces and bootlaces in a dozen different colors. Not one pair had a price tag under $6.99.

"Sweetie?" Mom called from the front of the shop. "I'm done here."

I followed her out, thinking, *I need cash. Lots of it.*

I took a deep breath and held my head high. If Mom could be a take-charge person, so could I. I'd just have to earn that money all by myself.

Chapter Three

Eddie was still moping in front of the TV when we came home. Mom put me in charge of dinner. She carried the licorice whips into the family room. I opened and closed kitchen cupboards. My ears strained to hear the conversation in the family room. So far nobody was talking. Were they being quiet because they were hugging, or was this an angry silence?

Not knowing the answer to that question killed my appetite. I gazed inside the refrigerator. Clear plastic bags of fresh vegetables gazed back. Still no sound from the family room. I pulled out the lettuce and cherry tomatoes. Finally, loving mumbles drifted into the kitchen. All my tight muscles softened. Mom and Eddie were speaking to each other. But we were still poor. I cooked a cheap meal of macaroni and cheese to go with the salad.

Over dinner Mom said, "Let's not look so glum, guys. We can make this work with a few adjustments. Eddie, if you and Poppy e-mailed each other instead of talking long distance, that would help."

Poppy (that was what we called Eddie's dad) lived in Maine. I glanced at Eddie. He just chewed and watched his plate.

"And we could cut the utilities bill if you only played non-electric instruments from now on," Mom said in her sunny voice. "You've got the piano in the living room, your acoustic guitar, saxophone—"

"I know what acoustic instruments I own, thank you," Eddie muttered.

His tone put me on alert. Mom and Eddie almost never argued, but I still remembered how scary it was ages ago when my real dad lived with us. Just the idea of a screaming match made my head go dizzy.

"I'm just saying we need to conserve," Mom began.

The macaroni noodles in my stomach bounced into each other. A fight was definitely brewing.

"Not necessarily," Eddie cut in. "Simon needs a new drummer. I can sub for him till he finds somebody permanent."

Mom put down her fork. She folded her hands under her chin. "Simon Jenner?" she asked Eddie from across the table. "I don't think so."

"Why not?" he said with big innocent eyes.

"I'm only going to say this once," Mom said. She lowered her arms.

When Mom said she'd only say something once, it meant rough times ahead.

"What would that be, dear?" Eddie said in a tight voice.

My insides tried to braid themselves into an SOS flag.

"Bad combination. You've given up—" Mom cut herself off. Her eyes moved toward me, then back to Eddie. I think that's the universal parental symbol for "let's talk in code," because the next thing she said was, "Simon plays you-know-where."

I didn't know where, but I was afraid to ask.

"It's extra money," said Eddie.

"Bad combination," she said with a head shake.

"I thought you were only allowed to say that once," said Eddie.

The flag in my gut started flapping. A huge fight was probably only two words away now. If I didn't fix this soon, the macaroni I ate would abandon ship.

"Mom, you play drums," I said. "Why don't *you* join Simon's band?"

Eddie laughed, but it wasn't a happy sound. We all knew he was a better drummer than she was. That made the laugh sound mean.

"Nobody's playing drums for Simon," Mom said.

"How about playing at weddings?" I asked.

"Thank you, Asa. You hear that, Lynne? I could play weddings."

Mom frowned. "And what do they serve at weddings?"

We didn't plan it. Eddie and I both said, "Cake."

"You know what I meant," said Mom.

Eddie shot a fiery stare at her. "You said you'd only mention it once. That's the third time."

My face pinched up in confusion. What exactly did Mom mention three times? "Eddie, come on," she said in sweet voice. "You don't need a silly old band anyway. There's a new lawyer in my building who needs a part-time secretary. I'll work a few extra hours. Asa can help around the house more. Won't you, sweetie?" she said, smiling at me.

I nodded.

"See?" said Mom. Her face turned sunny. "Problem solved. I'll pick up the slack with a little overtime. I don't mind."

"It's not the slack," Eddie said. He puffed out a big sigh and shook his head. "It's not the slack," he said again, this time in a sad voice.

"You miss the orchestra," I murmured, feeling bad for him. I remembered how rotten I'd felt last year when it got too expensive for me to take gymnastics class. It's hard to give up something you love.

"Too bad you don't know anybody who could get you a grant," said Mom.

"Or a fund-raiser," I said. In that instant an idea popped into my head. "Bake sale!" I cried out. I imagined a folding table filled with pink frosted cupcakes.

"I'm a musician," Eddie said, chasing a cherry tomato around his salad bowl with his fork. "I'm not selling baked goods."

Okay, so it wouldn't work for Eddie, but it made perfect sense for me. If I could sell a few dozen cupcakes I'd have my shoes in no time. *"I* should have a bake sale!"

Mom reached out and patted my shoulder. "Sweetie, you don't have to make money for the family. We're not that bad off."

"Lynnie's right," Eddie said in a friendly voice. "We're not bad off at all. I didn't make *that* much extra with the orchestra gig. It's more about losing the friendships and the music."

"Oh, lovey," Mom said. She leaped up and gave Eddie a hug from behind. While she was cooing over him, I excused myself. Acting lovey-dovey was a zillion times better than fighting, but I still didn't want to watch it.

I scurried down the hall to Eddie's study to make a bake sale call. I would have gone to my room if I had my own phone. Now that we were poor that would never happen.

I settled into Eddie's swivel chair and reached for his violin-shaped phone. I punched in Claire Migliore's number. Claire's my best friend. Plus, she cooks.

"Hello?" Claire's voice answered.

"Want to help me with a bake sale?" I said into the phone.

"I didn't know you belonged to any clubs that did bake sales."

"It's for me. I'm selling cupcakes in front of the grocery store for cash."

There was a long silence on the other end. I figured Claire was thinking. She was a big thinker.

"Don't you need a permit for that?" she said finally. Claire was honest to an annoying degree. She wouldn't even pull the tags off pillows that she owned.

"Girl Scouts don't use permits," I pointed out. "Nobody stops them when they sell cookies in front of the Acme."

"They're Girl Scouts. That's a nonprofit organization."

"What about a lemonade stand?" I said. "You don't need a permit for that. Would you help if I had a lemonade stand? Except instead of lemonade, we'll sell cupcakes."

"You can sell whatever you want in front of your own house," she said. "You just can't do it on commercial property."

"I can't sell cupcakes in front of my own house!" I protested. "Mom would ask questions. She's not supposed to know why I need the money."

"Why *do* you need the money?" Claire asked.

I filled her in on the Silhouette Racing Shoes and the colored laces. I even invited her to join The Fad with me.

"Okay, Asa, here's the thing about stupid fads. They're stupid."

I frowned and twisted the phone cord around my finger.

Best friends are supposed to be on your side when you want to join fads. Then I remembered something.

"Are you still mad at Jennifer and her friends for calling you Princess String Bean in sixth grade?" I asked. That was the year Claire grew taller than everybody in our class.

"I just don't want to be part of a clique that's full of back-stabbers, that's all," Claire said. "Why would anybody want to join their fad anyway?"

"It has to do with being popular for a few seconds before we turn anonymous again in high school."

Claire sighed into the phone.

"Can't you at least help a desperate friend make some money?" I asked. "It doesn't have to be cupcakes."

Another puffing sound came through the line. "Okay, but this is under protest." There was another pause while Claire thought it over. "Forget cupcakes," she said. "You'd waste half the money on ingredients. Daddy says if you want to become a millionaire, you have to find something that's free and sell it. Like ice."

Claire's dad was a dentist, not a millionaire. Still, he made an interesting point. I actually did have something I didn't need. In fact, I owned dozens of that something.

"Tote bags!" I cried out.

They had started accumulating when I got on a book club mailing list a few years ago. Pretty soon a whole bunch of other book clubs from all over the place were inviting me to join. They didn't know I was only ten. But Mom knew. So whenever my introductory books came, she'd catch me and make me return them. At least she let me keep the free tote bags the clubs gave away. I always wondered what I'd do with them.

"Okay, we're selling tote bags!" I said into the phone.

"Meet me in half an hour in front of the student union at Ram's Head College."

"Today?" Claire squealed. "I just got my hair cut."

I slumped against Eddie's desktop. Claire suffered from The Curse of the New Haircut. Her hairdresser always snipped too much and made her think her face looked bigger. That included her nose, which she swore was a honker.

It took twenty "pleases" and another fifty "your nose is fines," before she agreed to meet me.

I dashed to my room. First I did some fancy work with magic markers to hide the book club logos on the tote bags. Next I crammed the whole collection into my backpack. I zipped through the dining area toward the garage door. Mom was washing the dishes in the sink. Eddie was drying. I stopped with my hand on the doorknob and frowned at them.

"You mean we can't use the dishwasher either?"

"Where are you going?" Mom asked.

"I'm meeting Claire. Back in a few hours."

"Be back in one," Mom said. "I need to study tonight and I don't want to be worrying about you getting run over or something."

I grumbled to myself. Out loud I said, "Okay."

Claire and her bike were waiting for me in front of the marble student union sign. Her dark hair looked almost shorter than a boy's. I pretended not to notice. Her nose did stick out a little more. I sure didn't tell her *that.*

"We don't have much time, so we'd better get started." I set down my pack and opened it. "Good thing we're doing this now. Summer session's almost over. All the students will be gone in a week." I knew the Ram's Head College schedule since Eddie taught music there.

Claire nudged me with a pointy elbow. "Customers," she mumbled.

Three laughing college girls headed our way.

"What's our sales pitch?" Claire asked.

"Charity," I said out of the corner of my mouth.

Claire gaped at me. "We can't say that!"

"But it's for the needy. I really, *really* need those shoes."

I jumped in front of the lead girl. She paused at the building's stone steps.

"Excuse me," I said in my best salesperson voice. "How would you like to help the needy and yourself at the same time?"

The lead girl folded her arms. "So what are you selling?"

"Tote bags." I held them up by the handles. "We have a variety of colors and sizes to choose from. Everybody needs a tote bag."

"Not only that," Claire added, "but your small donation is tax deductible."

I wasn't sure what that meant, but it sounded good.

A girl with glasses opened her backpack and took out a change purse. "That navy one looks okay," she said. "How much?"

Claire and I blinked at each other. We hadn't thought that far ahead. Who knew what tote bags went for on the open market?

"Three bucks?" I said.

"She meant to say one," Claire said.

"One dollar?" asked the lead girl. "That's not too bad. You said it's for a worthy cause, right?" She fished her wallet from her backpack.

I nodded. "Your donations will help buy shoes for the poor."

"That's so nice," said the third girl. "I'll take two."

They strolled up the Student Union steps swinging my tote bags.

"Tell your friends we're selling tote bags for the needy," I called after them.

"Look at that!" Claire said, riffling through the cash. "We just made four dollars in under a minute."

I squinted at her. "It could've been twelve."

She gave an indignant sniff. "You're not *that* needy."

But Claire was wrong. I truly was that needy. Claire didn't know Eddie had lost his conducting job. I kept that to myself in case it was one of those family things Mom didn't want outsiders to know about.

We strolled across campus, peddling my colorful collection of tote bags. We had just passed the ten-dollar mark when we noticed a couple of bulky campus security guys eyeing us suspiciously. I guess they thought we belonged to some kind of cult. They started walking in our direction.

"You think it's illegal to sell tote bags on a college campus?" Claire whispered.

"I don't know, but it doesn't look like they want to buy one. Come on. Let's go."

Sure they were following us, we ducked into the library. We bolted into the ladies' room and cowered together in a stall. Claire wanted to flush away the last three tote bags. If we destroyed the evidence, she reasoned, the campus police couldn't arrest us for selling stuff. But I figured we could save the plumbing by tossing the bags in the wastebasket by the sink.

I shoved them into the trashcan opening. Now all we had to do was sneak out a back window. We examined the cinder block walls for a window to crawl through. All we found was an exhaust fan.

Claire huffed. "This is terrible. How are you supposed to escape if there's a fire?"

"Never go to the bathroom if you smell smoke," I said. "Come on."

We tiptoed back to the door. I eased it open wide enough for my right eye to peek through. I didn't see any big guys waiting for us. I let the door swing shut and turned to Claire. "On three," I whispered, "we'll walk briskly through the lobby and out the main door. If anybody yells, we'll pretend we can't hear."

Claire nodded.

I looked outside again. "One…"

"Three!" Claire shrieked. She shoved me out the door.

We walked so briskly some might call it running. Fortunately nobody yelled at us. Nobody followed either. We didn't know if the security guys lost interest or if they went to get the campus police. We didn't wait to find out. We raced across campus to our bikes.

At the first intersection Claire pedaled straight, toward her house. I turned right.

Back home, Mom was studying her paralegal stuff at the dining table. Eddie played "Bridge Over Troubled Waters" on the piano. I locked myself in my room.

I pulled an old bank envelope out of my desk drawer. The money tucked inside equaled forty-two dollars and fifty-eight cents. With the ten from the tote-bag sale, the total was over fifty dollars. School was only a month away. That meant I needed another moneymaking scheme. Fast.

Chapter Four

The phone rang just before two on Friday afternoon. Mom was at work. Eddie was probably around somewhere, but I hadn't seen him. I took the call on the violin phone. It was Mrs. Petrie, Abby's mom.

"Yesterday morning I dressed Abigail in a pink sunsuit," her crisp, businesslike voice said. "When I came in last night she was wearing green shorts and a yellow top."

Pink sunsuit. The words sent an electric jolt through me. I couldn't remember what I did with Abby's pink sunsuit.

Think, think.

I always used a four-step plan to save Abby's picky mom from knowing her kid actually got dirty. It went like this:

Step 1—Get Abby out of muddy clothes.

Step 2—Wash clothes in bathroom sink.

Step 3—Throw clothes in dryer.

Step 4—Put freshly laundered clothes back on Abby.

The plan had always worked. Until now. I was so excited yesterday about the latest fad that I'd only completed step one. Oops.

"Imagine my dismay," Mrs. Petrie said, "when I discovered my little girl's pink sunsuit just now in the sink in the guest bathroom. It is absolutely covered in filth. Where did you take her? On an outing to a pig sty?"

I tried to squeeze in an explanation, but Mrs. Petrie's words plowed over mine. What kind of a sitter would allow a child's clothes to become so soiled? Why wasn't I supervising Abigail properly? Was I entertaining boys at her house instead of performing my duties as a sitter?

"I don't have a boyfriend!" I shouted into the phone.

"You don't have a job either," she snapped back. "Abigail and I no longer require your services." The phone clicked dead in my ear.

I sat in a daze. Fired. Just like that. What would poor little Abby think tomorrow morning when her favorite mud pie baby-sitter didn't show up? I knew she liked me. Maybe she'd throw a tantrum and I'd get my job back. I sure did need cash.

Cash! It suddenly dawned on me that I'd just lost my shoe-money job. I pounced on the phone's keypad and punched in Claire's number for more moneymaking advice. But she wasn't home. Her mom said Claire was at a cousin's sleepover birthday party.

I tried my second best friend, Joy Stewart. Sometimes she had better ideas than Claire. Joy was what my mom called a go-getter. She didn't even mind a little dishonesty if it got the job done.

Joy wasn't home either. At least she was expected back soon. I left a message.

The full force of my getting fired started to sink in now. I hadn't just lost the extra money. Abby's mom didn't trust me anymore. I slumped against the back of the chair and groaned. It was so unfair. I was a good baby-sitter. No, I was a great baby-sitter. Even Jennifer Terrell said so. I didn't just play in mud with Abby, I always cooked her favorite lunch, macaroni and cheese. When she wanted something sweet, I only gave her bananas and raisins. I read her stories and made sure she took her nap. I sang to her. Abby's mom should've been calling to give me a raise! Instead, I got kicked out of Abby's life. I choked back a few tears. Why wasn't anybody ever around when I needed to hear some comforting words? Then I remembered there was at least one loving person as close as the phone. I reached for it again.

After four rings Mom's rushed voice said, "Law offices, please hold." Next came the elevator music. She didn't even ask who I was first! Obviously, she was too busy to give me any sympathy. I hung up before she came back on the line.

I scuffed to the kitchen for a glass of orange juice. Anything to take my mind off my misery.

Soft guitar music played from the family room.

Eddie! He knew how it felt to lose a job. Maybe he could make me feel better. I poked my head through the doorway to the family room.

My stepdad sat on the edge of the couch with an acoustic guitar in his lap. The coffee table in front of him was covered with manuscript paper. Some of it was rolled into balls. The rest was either blank or scribbled on.

"Composing?" I asked.

Eddie kept strumming. "Trying to," he said, not looking up. "Tune's there, but the words aren't coming." He lifted his head. "What's wrong with you? You look like your dog just died."

We didn't even own a dog, but I still felt like crying. I tried to look brave. "I just got fired for making mud pies with Abigail."

That kind of news would make a real dad look sad from sympathy. A real dad would have said, "You poor kid." A real dad would've offered me a hug.

Eddie's face lit up. "Mud pies with Abigail!" he said excitedly. "That's it! Mind if I use that?"

He didn't even wait for an answer. Eddie hunched over his manuscript paper. He scribbled so fast I didn't think his brain had time to tell his hand what to write. That's the way it is with musical geniuses sometimes. They get so lost in the music they forget about the people who need them.

I sighed and turned away. I was on my own again. Halfway down the hall the phone rang. I answered it in Eddie's study again. It was Joy.

"Abby?" Joy said after I told her the whole sad story of getting fired. "Isn't that the kid who lives next door to Jennifer Terrell?"

"Yes." I sighed. "Thank you for taking an interest. When I told Eddie, all he did was ask if he could write a song about my pain."

Joy chuckled. "If you poked that guy with a fork I bet musical notes would squirt out."

"I'd like to poke him with a fork," I muttered.

Since Joy hated fads more than Claire did, I only said I needed new ideas for generating quick cash. I didn't tell her what the cash was for.

"Ooh, ooh!" Joy said. She sounded like a kid waving her hand to show the teacher she knew the answer. "Garage sale!"

Joy was supposed to be more creative than Claire. Right now I wasn't so sure. Did people actually buy the stuff other people put out at garage sales? "Uh, really?" I said.

"Definitely. Don't you remember last year when Liz and I had one? We made two hundred bucks just selling old toys and clothes and stuff."

I wished I had a big sister to help me with a garage sale.

But for that to work Mom and Eddie would have to adopt. That was highly unlikely. I let out a disappointed sigh.

"Of course, we had to give most of the money back to Dad," Joy added. "We accidentally sold his snow tires for twenty-five dollars."

I thanked her for the tip and hung up. Maybe a garage sale wasn't such a bad idea after all. I had tons of junk I didn't use any more. Plus, I'd never sell Eddie's snow tires. All I needed was permission. I raced back to the family room. I hoped Eddie was done writing songs about dirt so I could ask.

Before my lips formed the first word, Eddie looked up and smiled at me.

"Listen to this," he said.

His slender fingers danced over the guitar strings. He plucked sweet notes and strummed pretty chords. My head bobbed to the catchy rhythm. Then he began to sing. It was the first time he'd ever sung for me without using a funny accent.

He had a gentle voice, one full of feeling. If he sang a love song, you'd believe it.

Eddie's new song wasn't about love or dirt. It was about a guy remembering when he was young and free. Mud pies never came into the lyrics. He didn't even use the name Abigail.

On the surface the tune and the words sounded happy, but I got the meaning buried inside. The guy in the song wasn't young anymore. Even though he didn't say it, you got the feeling all his good times were over. That made the song seem sad.

"Wow," was all I could say when he finished.

Eddie peered up at me. He looked like a shy little kid showing off his first finger painting. "Like it?"

I stared at him. Like it? He'd just written a song that belonged on the radio and he'd done it in five minutes flat!

"I didn't know you were, you know, so…good."

Eddie's cheeks dimpled. He shrugged and looked down. "I've been told I have my moments."

"Wish I could play like that," I said honestly.

He looked up again, all smiles. "You can, Ace! If you're interested, I've got an old guitar or two around here somewhere."

"Okay," I said.

He put down his own guitar and trotted out of the room. It wasn't till I heard him rooting around in a back closet that I started to have doubts. I saw myself more as a tambourine kind of person. I didn't think I was coordinated enough to play guitar. You had to pinch down on the strings with one hand and strum with the other. Kind of like rubbing your stomach and patting your head at the same time. While Eddie thumped and bumped in the closet, I tested my coordination. I kept patting and rubbing the wrong way.

Okay, it didn't look like I'd make a million bucks as a rock star. Good thing I had another money scheme.

"Um, can I have a garage sale?" I called to Eddie.

From the back of the house I heard a musical, "No, no, no."

Eddie returned a few moments later with a dusty case. "Here we are," he said.

The old guitar looked dingy next to the shiny one he played now. My shoulders drooped a little. I wanted a guitar that looked so flashy nobody would realize I couldn't play it.

Eddie started to tune the old guitar. "This'll be fun," he said. "I was about your age when I took up the guitar."

I forced a smile. The difference between Eddie learning the guitar at thirteen and me learning was that he had been a child prodigy on piano since age six. I couldn't even play a tune on a comb and wax paper. This was all probably a very bad idea, but Eddie looked so happy I didn't want to spoil the mood.

"Here we go," he said finally, handing over the ugly guitar. He swung his own onto his lap. "This is an A chord," he said. Eddie pressed his first three fingers over the three middle strings toward the top of the neck and strummed. "You know it wasn't about the money, Ace," he said suddenly.

I frowned. What was he talking about?

His fingers slid down the fret and played another chord. "Losing the orchestra," he went on. "Never was. It's about being on stage." He looked up from his guitar. "Your mom doesn't get that part. That's why she'll never perform in a band. She thinks of her drum practice as some kind of aerobic exercise."

I didn't answer. I wasn't sure what to say.

"Now you try the A chord," Eddie instructed. "Next fret up," he added gently, easing my fingers into the right position. "Give it a strum."

I strummed, but my chord sounded fuzzy.

"Press down harder on the strings, Ace."

When I did, the strings dug into the balls of my fingers. "Yow!" I snatched my hand away. My fingers had stripes dented into them. "I bet this is how a hard-boiled egg feels when you put it through an egg slicer."

Eddie laughed. "Nah. You know what you need?" he said.

"Leather gloves?"

He chuckled. "Vinyl strings. They're not as hard on the fingers."

39

"Maybe you should teach me to play the tambourine."

"No, this'll be fun. We'll get you some new strings." He shot off the couch. "Come on, kiddo, road trip to the Ram's Head Music Store."

My fingers still stung from playing one chord. I didn't want to play guitar anymore, but Eddie and I were actually getting along. I shook out my hand and followed him to the car. Pulling out of the garage reminded me why I'd gone to Eddie in the first place.

"Why can't I have that garage sale?" I asked. "I could earn us extra money."

Eddie glanced at me. "First off," he said, focusing on the driveway, "we don't need extra money. Your mom's already taking care of that with overtime. And second, I don't want strangers in my garage, pawing over my stuff."

"All I'll be selling is old toys. *My* old toys."

"Nope."

That ended the conversation. And my plan. I couldn't ask Mom. If I did she'd want to know why I needed the cash. If she knew about the Silhouette Racing Shoes she'd remind me I'm supposed to be my own woman.

At the music shop I hung back from Eddie. I stared up at all the flashy guitars hanging on the left wall. Maybe if I found one I liked I'd actually want to learn to play and make him happy. That's when I saw the shiny one in robin's egg blue. It looked like a bent triangle. My eyes zoomed in on the price. Five hundred and ninety-nine dollars. My mouth dropped open. Mom would have to work over-overtime to afford that.

"Edward-o!" Chester called from behind the counter.

I turned from the guitar display. I knew Chester from

watching community orchestra rehearsals. He played percussion. I liked his ponytail. It went all the way down his back.

"Your ears must be burning, bro," said Chester. "I was just talking about you."

Eddie grinned. "I wanted to talk to you, too." He stepped up to the counter and leaned his elbows on the glass.

They bent their heads together and started whispering.

I had two choices. I could stay where I was and concentrate on thinking up a better argument for my garage sale, or inch closer to spy on the big secret going on at the counter. Curiosity won. Two baby steps later Eddie said, "Ace, why don't you go get some 5Bs for your mom?"

Chester smiled and winked at me.

My brain groaned to itself. The drumsticks were a zillion miles from the counter. If I wanted to catch any of the conversation, I'd have to hurry. I tore down the aisle to the rack that held the different sticks. Technically you were supposed to roll them first to make sure they weren't warped. I just snatched the first pair of 5B sticks I saw and rushed back.

Too late. They weren't talking together anymore. Eddie had moved behind the counter. He had his back to me and his ear pressed against the store telephone. He was mumbling something into the mouthpiece.

"Find 'em okay, Ace?" asked Chester.

I nodded. "What's he doing?" I jerked my head toward Eddie.

"Phone," was all Chester said. He rang up the vinyl strings and drumsticks. "Gonna take up the guitar, are ya, Ace?"

"Guess so. Did Eddie get a phone call here?" I asked.

Chester chucked me under the chin. "You heard what curiosity did to the cat, didn't you?"

"Yeah, but—"

At that moment Eddie hung up and turned around. "All set, Chester. Thanks."

Eddie paid for the drumsticks and loped outside to the car. I followed. I had no choice.

"Was that Mom on the phone?" I asked in the car.

"Business," he said. "By the way, we're taking a little detour, Ace."

My fingers were happy they didn't have to play the ugly guitar yet, but I didn't have time for detours. I needed to make shoe money.

Eddie drove us out of town. We passed some farmland and a couple of little towns. He drove up a woodsy hill. At the top, he turned onto a narrow drive. The road wound its way through the forest to a gravel parking lot. A shabby sign hung in front of a log cabin. The sign read, "Cappy's Tavern."

A shiver rattled through me. I turned to Eddie. "What kind of detour is this?" I asked. The place looked like a bar. He ignored me and popped out of the car. I hurried after him.

It was cool and dim inside. It stank from cigarette smoke and old greasy fried food. My jumpy stomach told me I didn't belong here. I wasn't sure Eddie did, either.

A gravelly laughing noise came from the old guy behind the bar. He had a doughy face and a big belly. "Why, looky here what the cat done drug in!"

"Eddo!" cried two wrinkly faced guys from their bar stools. Smoke from their cigarettes formed a gray cloud above their end of the bar. I shrank behind Eddie. Sure, the old guys seemed friendly enough, but this didn't feel like a good place to be.

"The two Robs!" Eddie greeted them. He laughed and stomped his foot. "Seven years and you're still in the same spot."

"You should've been here last week," said the Rob on the left. "We sat down there." He pointed to the opposite end of the bar.

Eddie cracked up laughing.

"Who ya got with ya?" asked the other Rob. His voice was kind of slurry.

Eddie wrapped his arm around my shoulders and pulled me next to him. "This is Asa Marie. Don't mind if my kid plays a little pinball, do you, Cap?" he asked the bartender.

Whoa. His kid? He called me his kid! Did that mean I was supposed to call him Dad now?

The bartender's piggy eyes widened. He looked from me to Eddie. "You got a kid now? Has it been that long?"

"She's only six. Tall for her age," Eddie said. He laughed and guided me toward an old space-alien pinball machine. He slapped a handful of quarters onto the glass top. "Start 'er up, Ace. Two players. I'll get us a drink."

My insides rumbled. I slid the quarters into the slot with a wobbly hand. Mom was going to kill us. She still had a booze phobia from growing up with her own dad who was an alcoholic. She used to tell me her dad spent all his free time in bars. That's where all the lowlifes went to quench their thirst. According to Mom.

The pinball machine chirped and pinged to life.

Eddie handed me a fizzy cola. I took a sip and eyed the glass in his hand.

"What?" he said innocently. "It's just a little orange juice. You know, vitamin C? Sunshine in a glass."

He clinked his glass against mine. Eddie took a sip of juice and set the glass on the table by the pinball machine. He rubbed his hands together. "Be prepared for slaughter, Ace, I'm good at this."

The silver ball banged against the bumpers and flappers. Red and yellow lights winked on and off. Alien noises squeaked and burbled from the speakers. I focused on the game. I almost forgot about the smoke smells and Mom's bar stories.

The game was a blast! Soon we were laughing and teasing each other. We jostled elbows, trying to break each other's concentration. On Eddie's turn I blocked his view of the ball with my hands. On mine he said, "Hey, look over there on the floor! A twenty-dollar bill!" The whole time our scores clicked upward.

For a minute or two I knew how Claire must feel, playing Ping-Pong with her dad. Or why Joy liked to play basketball in the driveway with her dad. Kids played with their dads. And here I was, for practically the first time in six years, playing a game with Eddie.

His ball hit bumper after bumper, scoring bonus points. I nudged him to try to make him miss. When that didn't work I said, "Whoa, an alien just walked in!"

Somebody really had come through the door. It wasn't an alien, though. It was a tall, skinny guy with frizzy hair and a blond beard.

Eddie looked up. Frizzy Guy nodded at him. Eddie's ball rolled between the flappers. He didn't even try to stop it.

"Take over for me, okay?" he said to me. Then Eddie turned and ambled toward Frizzy Guy. They shook hands and slid onto stools at the bar, away from the two Robs.

I just stared at them with my mouth open. That wasn't how it was supposed to work. Claire's dad never quit on her in the middle of a Ping-Pong match. Joy and her dad kept shooting hoops till they spelled H-O-R-S-E.

I checked the scoreboard. Eddie was ahead by 50,000 points. I had two balls to catch up, but it didn't matter anymore. What was the point of competing when your dad already quit? Non-dad, I corrected. I slumped against the machine.

Across the room Eddie ordered another orange juice. The bartender added something from one of his bottles. The liquid looked clear. I knew it wasn't spring water. I muttered a word I'm not allowed to call people. I turned back to the pinball machine and pulled the lever. Three games later Eddie gave me a nudge.

Nobody talked on the ride home. I knew Eddie was up to something. It had started at the music shop and kept going with Frizzy Guy. Just thinking about whatever it was made my heart bounce to an angry beat.

I felt like the grown-up. Eddie was the kid who said he was going to the library but played video games at a friend's house instead. To make it worse, he was starting to whistle right now, as if nothing at all was the matter.

My insides pulsed. I couldn't make myself say it out loud, but I knew. Eddie was up to something bad. My mom wouldn't like it. And neither did I.

Chapter Five

Eddie and I didn't talk that night even though we cooked dinner together. Maybe it was because we worked in separate places. I was in charge of boiling the brussels sprouts and Pennsylvania Dutch noodles in the kitchen. Eddie barbecued chicken outside. Neither of us spoke even after he brought the yummy-smelling chicken inside. Maybe we were just hungry. Two minutes into the meal, Mom shot through the garage door.

"Sorry I'm late," she said, puffing. She kicked off her shoes and dropped into her chair in the kitchen. "Last-minute hassles at work. But everything looks fabulous. Thanks, guys."

She reached near me for the noodle bowl. She sniffed the air. "Why do I smell smoke?"

Eddie sat upright. "Is my grill on fire?"

"I meant cigarette smoke," Mom said. She frowned and leaned closer toward me. She sniffed again. "Have you been smoking, Asa Marie?"

"Me?" I said, insulted. "No way!"

"Don't be silly, Lynnie," Eddie cut in. "We were together the whole day. She never even touched a match."

"But she reeks of cigarettes."

Oh no! I had forgotten that cigarette smoke sticks to material. I squinted at Eddie. He'd taken a shower the minute we got back from the bar. He'd even done a load of laundry. Now he smelled like fresh clothes and sweet soap.

"Oh, *that*," Eddie said in a jolly voice. "I know what it is. We saw Ben today. You know how he puffs like a smokestack. We spent some time at his place discussing fund-raising ideas. You know," he added with a shrug. "Trying to bring back the orchestra."

Mom's face lit up immediately. "That's terrific!"

"If it works it will be."

I almost choked on a brussels sprout. Eddie's fib came out so naturally I almost believed him. He was a better liar than Joy Stewart.

But Joy's made-up stories were funny. I didn't feel like laughing at Eddie's. He was supposed to be a *dad*, not a liar.

"Lynnie," said Eddie, "while we were out we bought you some new sticks."

Mom stopped smiling. "Aren't we supposed to be saving money?"

If she was going to yell at Eddie this time, I didn't mind. I just kept thinking, *Ha! Serves you right, Edward C. Clegg, you big fat liar.*

After dinner he ducked into his study. Mom went down to the basement to practice her drums. Without the new sticks. They were supposed to go straight back to the store tomorrow. Soon her warm-up exercises clickity-clacked up through the floor. I inched down the hall toward the study. Eddie sat at his desk, facing his computer. His fingers galloped over the keyboard. He typed even faster than he played piano.

I waited in the doorway.

Finally, he turned his head toward me. "Need to use the computer?"

I frowned back. "You lied to my mom."

Even though she couldn't hear us over her own noise, Eddie said in a quiet voice, "Come in, Ace. Close the door."

I wanted to slam it. I wanted to scream. But Mom would've heard a noise that loud. I shut the door with a gentle click. This was between Eddie and me.

"You lied," I said again through clenched teeth.

Eddie shrugged. "So did you."

"What?"

"You didn't tell your mom where we went either."

I just gaped at him. Was he serious? Of course I didn't tell Mom! She'd divorced my real dad because he drank too much. I still remembered getting dressed with her before her wedding to Eddie. She leaned close to me, all frills and perfume, and whispered the biggest promise in the world: "No more drunks in our life, Asa Marie."

"Look at it this way, Ace. What good would it do upsetting your mom? Right? Besides, I just e-mailed Ben." Eddie jabbed his thumb at his computer. "About fund-raisers. Do you know what Ben does when he isn't playing tympani?"

I shook my head. I really didn't care.

"Performs at birthday parties as a clown."

I folded my arms and shifted my weight. I didn't see how clowns could help us if Eddie was turning into a drunk.

"For a living!" Eddie said, full of enthusiasm. "Obviously the guy knows something about marketing if he can do that. He can help us. So I didn't lie to your mom. We really are working on it."

It still felt like a lie to me. I stared at the floor. *No more drunks in our life.*

"Look, Ace, if you want to get technical, I didn't do any-thing wrong. Your mom said I shouldn't play in Simon's band. The guy I met today is named Randy."

I looked up. "Is that who you were talking to on the phone at the music shop?"

He nodded. "Chester gave me the tip. I had to set up the meeting right away."

So Eddie had met Frizzy Guy—Randy—on purpose. I scowled and looked away. Eddie hadn't taken me to the bar to play pinball. He just needed to kill time till Frizzy Randy showed up for their meeting.

"Ace, come on. It's not like I killed a puppy."

But he drank today even though Mom thought he had quit. I was sure of it. I took a deep breath and tried to figure this out. Could one trip to a bar make you a drunk like my grandpa?

"I'm just trying to get a little extra work," Eddie went on. "Randy needs a bass player. I play bass. I'm helping the family."

We were back to his stupid buddy, Randy. I shrugged and pretended I didn't care. So what if Eddie liked Frizzy Randy's band more than he liked me? It didn't matter.

"Ace, I'll make a deal with you," Eddie said. "You don't tell your mom about Randy's band and I'll let you have your garage sale."

My garage sale! I'd almost forgotten about needing money for shoes. My heart beat faster than Mom's drums. "Really?"

"Just keep everybody out of my garage, okay? We'll call it a yard sale. And don't sell anything that's mine. Deal?"

Part of me started mentally counting the money I'd make.

Another part rumbled with Mom's tom-toms. It would be wrong to hide the truth from my own mother. I had to think about this. Did I want money for The Fad or did I want to tell Mom the truth? My heart pounded harder. I raised my head. "Deal."

Eddie grinned. His eyes sparkled. He even winked at me.

I spun on my heel and galloped out of the room. Eddie didn't call me back. I raced through the house to the garage door and burst outside. I stood alone in the driveway, gulping for air. A hot pulse whooshed through my ears. Why did I feel so guilty? I was just trying to earn some money.

I gazed across the wide, paved driveway our house shared with the Weber family. Eddie was right. He wasn't killing puppies; he just wanted to play in a band. And I wasn't exactly lying to Mom. I was saving her from getting upset. I was also saving her money by earning my own cash to buy school shoes.

The sun started to dip behind the trees. A chorus of crickets chirped, "Okay, okay, okay." I stood listening in the warm, summer air. Maybe the crickets were right. Everything would work out.

I zeroed in on two cars parked next door. The red one with dried mud on the front fender belonged to Jason, the Weber's sixteen-year-old son. The gray one with the bird droppings on the roof belonged to the mom. Suddenly, I came up with another sure-fire moneymaking scheme: Car wash! I marched next door and hired myself out at five bucks a car.

During the pre-rinse cycle I got the prickly feeling that the other Weber son, Little Domino, was spying on me from their hedge. I slapped a soapy sponge onto his mom's windshield. Mostly I called Domino "little" because it bugged him. Up until a month ago I was taller than he was. Now we were both five-feet-two. My birthday was three whole weeks before his. That made me more mature than him.

Domino came out of hiding. The length of his sun-bleached hair always told how deep into summer vacation we were. He let it grow over the summer. I did just the opposite. I kept my hair short till the fall, then let it grow out to keep my ears warm for winter.

Domino's bangs were in his eyes. His hair almost touched his shoulders. That meant I didn't have much time left to earn Silhouette and shoelace money before the first day of school.

Domino punched me in the arm in greeting. He always did that. "Way to go, Ace. Mom just sent me out here to help. How'd you talk her into paying you? She usually makes me and my brother do this for free. And why are you washing cars anyway?"

"I need to buy important stuff for school," I said.

Domino pinched up his face, exposing his chipped front tooth from an old bicycle accident. "Yeah? Like what?"

"You might not get it," I said. So far none of my other friends had.

"I was *this* close to making fifteenth level," he said, holding his thumb and index finger close together. "Then Mom made me come help you. Do you know how hard it is to get to fifteen?"

"You're only supposed to play video games when it rains," I pointed out.

"It *is* raining," he said with an evil grin.

Domino snatched the hose and squirted me. That started

a water battle. Next came the hose wrestling competition. We even had a sponge toss. Between events I tried to explain to Domino why I needed money.

"Jennifer will never let you in her group," Domino said on the final rinse.

Just as I suspected. He didn't get it either. That bugged me. I changed the subject by shooting water down his pants.

We grappled with the hose. A few minutes later a third car eased into Dom's side of the driveway. Domino let go of the hose. "Let's do my dad's car," he whispered. "Except we'll overcharge him!"

Mr. Weber, big as a football player, unfolded himself from the front seat. He grinned down at us. "What have we here?"

"Car wash," Domino said. "Interested?"

Mr. Weber's wide face brightened. "Sounds good."

"Ten bucks. Up front," Dom said.

His dad gave him a bear hug. "Ten bucks?" he said in a teasing voice. He rubbed his knuckles over the top of Dom's head. "Don't you mean free?"

"Nope," Dom said. He hugged his dad back. "Asa needs money."

Worry lines sprouted above Mr. Weber's blond eyebrows. "I'm sorry." he said in a softer voice. "I didn't realize…" He opened his wallet.

"It's no big deal," I blurted. Nobody in the neighborhood was supposed to know about our money problems. "I'm…uh, starting a hobby."

"A stupid hobby," Dom cut in.

"I don't *need* the money," I added quickly. " I just wanted to pay for my own, uh, hobby."

"Understood," Mr. Weber said with a nod. He doled out

fives to each of us. "Clean the inside while you're at it. Somebody ate popcorn in the backseat. I wonder who *that* was." He gave Dom a playful shove and ambled inside.

"You have a really great dad," I said.

Domino picked up the hose. "We should've asked for twenty."

I wanted to throw the sponge at him. Dom was so clueless. He had a dad who loved him and hugged him and gave him five-dollar bills even when he spilled popcorn in the backseat. Dom probably didn't even realize there were people in the world who didn't have a dad at all.

Like me.

That night I dreamed I was a little kid, maybe four or five. I felt scared, standing alone in an amusement park. I heard a roller coaster rattle on its tracks. People laughed in a loud, scary way. Crowds hustled by but all I saw were long legs, gliding past. My heart pounded harder. I shouted one name over and over. Nobody came to me. Nobody answered.

I woke up with tears on my cheeks.

The name I called was "Daddy."

Chapter Six

I couldn't afford a newspaper ad for my yard sale. Instead, Domino helped me tack up signs around the neighborhood. As payment, I let him join the sale. We surrounded ourselves with old bikes and sports equipment and boxes crammed with games and toys. We piled all the clothes we'd outgrown on a card table in my front yard. There must have been at least a hundred bucks worth of junk. We sat on lawn chairs and waited for customers.

A whole hour passed before a car rolled to our curb. Dom sold a baseball glove and a rusty bike for eight dollars. The car drove away.

"This is dumb," I grumbled.

"I hate to tell you, but this is a rotten neighborhood for yard sales," Domino said.

I glared at him. "Thanks for the warning ahead of time."

"Hey, if I get a big mowing job, want me to hire you?"

"How good's the pay?" I asked.

Domino smirked. "Better than this."

Claire, Joy, and Joy's eight-year-old sister Tammy coasted in on their bikes.

"Hey, Ace," Joy called out. "We've come to throw some business your way."

I leaped off my chair. "Hi! You guys don't really have to do this," I added, even though I didn't mean it. If strangers weren't going to buy my junk, friends with allowance money were the next best thing.

"Do you have any jigsaw puzzles?" Claire asked.

"Right this way," I said, and opened the nearest cardboard box. Claire knelt beside it. She carefully sorted through the selection.

Tammy pawed through another box. She held up a baby doll in a blue jumper. "I like her."

"That'll be a hundred bucks," said Domino. He held out his palm.

Tammy's shoulders drooped. "Really?"

I squinted at Dom.

"What?" he said, looking innocent. "It's the perfect plan. All you have to do is sell one thing."

"Funny," I muttered.

Tammy hugged the doll.

"We'll give you two dollars," said Joy.

"Four," I said.

"Three."

"Sold," I said.

Tammy bounced up and down. "Thank you, thank you, thank you!"

I merrily collected the payment from Joy.

"This is pretty," Claire said. She held up a puzzle box with a picture of a lighthouse on a snowy hill. "How much?"

"Puzzles are a dollar a piece," I said.

"Great! Then I'll get another one."

"She meant a hundred dollars a piece," Domino piped up.

"Dom, will you stop that?" I said.

"Whoa! Check this out!" Joy said. Half a dozen stuffed

animals lay tossed on the ground around her. She was holding up an 8 x 10 picture frame. Inside was an autographed
picture of Eddie, dressed as Mr. Music. I'd forgotten all about
that picture. I bet Mom had too. Maybe I could sell it to
Jennifer Terrell. She loved Mr. Music.

Tammy tucked her new doll under her arm and skipped
toward Joy. She peered at the picture. "Ace, is that your stepdad pretending to be a clown?"

"No, it's Mr. Music!" Joy sang out. She grinned at Eddie's
smiling face. "So, Mr. Music was Eddie. I always thought he
looked familiar." She looked up. "Why didn't you ever tell
me?"

I shrugged. The truth was, it had all happened so long ago
I forgot. Sort of. Besides, by the time Mom and Eddie got
married, he was just plain Eddie.

Claire stretched her long neck for a better look, then went
back to the box of puzzles. I guess she wasn't a big Mr. Music
fan. It was a relief to know at least one of my best friends had
the same tastes as me.

"Who is Mr. Music?" asked Tammy.

"Before your time," Joy said. "This clown named Looney
Clooney had a TV show when I was a little kid. Mr. Music
was his sidekick."

"Hey, I remember that show," said Dom. "That was
Eddie?"

"Come on, everybody," I said, getting disgusted. Was I the
only four-year-old in the whole world who *didn't* watch that
stupid show?

"Our big sister Liz saw the show in person once," Joy said
to Domino. "She went with her Girl Scout troop to a taping.

Remember how the camera used to focus on different kids in the studio audience?"

"Yeah," he answered.

I just shook my head. Why would anybody want to remember something that happened a zillion years ago?

"Well, get this," said Joy. "Liz wanted to be discovered by a talent scout so she wore a big green bow in her hair to attract attention. But it was too bad for her 'cause the show never aired. Mr. Music kept flubbing his lines!" Joy practically fell over backwards laughing.

I frowned at her. "Mr. Music didn't have any lines." At least I knew that much about the show. "He didn't talk."

Joy sprang to her feet, still gripping the frame. "I gotta buy this!"

"How could he flub his lines?" I said. At least Joy could get her facts straight. "He was the Mute Musician, remember?"

I didn't know a lot about Eddie's Looney Clooney days. All I knew was he hated wearing the Mr. Music suit and felt stupid signing autographs at the mall. But he always took his music seriously. He was a musician first.

"Mr. Music never made mistakes on TV," I said.

Joy sighed. "Never mind, Ace. What do you want for the picture?"

"A hundred bucks," Domino repeated.

I snatched the frame out of Joy's hands. "Mr. Music never flubbed his lines."

"Come on. Sell it to me, please?" Joy begged. "It'll kill Liz when she sees it. She still wants to be famous."

"It's not for sale," I said flatly.

Joy folded her arms and glared at me.

"He didn't flub," I mumbled.

Joy motioned to me. I followed her behind the maple tree in my front yard. "Okay, listen," she said in a whisper. "You want to know the real reason they never aired that Looney Clooney episode? Because Mr. Music was drunk. Okay? There, I said it. Happy now?"

"He w-was n-not," I sputtered. Mr. Music couldn't get drunk. Right before the wedding Mom had promised me. No more drunks in our lives.

Eddie might lie, but Mom never did. Mom never lied, but Joy did.

I set my jaw and stared hard at Joy. "You made that up."

She threw up her arms. "Are you nuts?" she said. "Why do you think they fired him? It was for being loaded on the set all the time."

"Stop it!" I cried. "He quit."

Joy shook her head. "Nope. My sister said she read about it in the newspaper. Or maybe it was a magazine."

"You're just saying that because I won't sell you the stupid picture."

"You don't believe me? Then ask Mr. Music yourself."

"Maybe I will," I snapped back. I tucked the frame under my arm and stomped across the yard to my back door.

I found Eddie in his usual place at his computer, pecking away at the computer keyboard.

"Report this to your mom," he said, when he noticed me in the doorway. "I'm sending an e-mail to Poppy. See? No long distance phone calls."

"Uh huh," I said.

He scanned the screen. "How'd you make out with the sale?"

"It's still kind of going on. So far Claire and Tammy are my best customers."

Eddie chuckled. "That's what friends are for, right?"

"Somebody wanted to buy this, but I wouldn't sell it." I held out the picture.

"Mmm-hmm. Be right with you, Ace." He typed a few more words and pressed the Send key.

I set the picture in front of his monitor, facing him. "Remember this?" I asked.

He cracked up laughing. "Man, did I really look that ridiculous?" Eddie lifted the picture. "Where'd you find it?"

"Basement. In one of the boxes I took to the sale."

"I remember giving this to your mom at the mall." He looked up. "Then we went to dinner. You were only about this high." Eddie held his free hand a few inches above his desk. "I kept feeding you quarters to go play the video game in the corner."

"To get rid of me," I said. "Like at the bar last week."

Eddie raised an eyebrow at that last part, then ignored it. "When you were small you were somewhat of a pest," he said. "Of course, I mean that in a loving way."

"You quit being Mr. Music because you didn't like all those piano keys on the suit, right?" I said. "You weren't fired."

His mouth turned serious. Then he narrowed his eyes. "Who said I got fired?"

"Joy."

"Has that kid suddenly become an expert on my life?" Eddie threw up his hands. "What's she doing, writing my biography on the side?"

"Joy doesn't have a good day unless she gets in about twenty lies," I said.

Eddie carefully put down the picture. "I wasn't fired, Ace. You can tell her that. I have never been fired from a job. I quit."

I nodded, feeling better already. "That's what I thought," I said. "You quit 'cause you hated the outfit."

"I hated that outfit all right." He gazed at the picture and his eyes got a faraway look. I waited for him to come back.

It took a minute or two. When Eddie moved again it was to reach for the mug on his desk. He turned and dumped the old coffee into the potted plant behind him. "Do me a favor, Ace. You know that bottle in your closet? Pour a nip into this, please."

I froze. I couldn't even blink. That bottle in my closet wasn't for drinking. Eddie told me months ago it was just a reminder that silly people gave silly Christmas presents. Mom still didn't know it was there.

"I…don't think Mom would like you…uh, nipping."

"Mom isn't here," he said quietly.

I bowed my head. Mom wasn't there when Eddie started hiding things either.

When we moved into Eddie's house after the wedding, nobody drank. Then just this past Christmas the first bottle showed up. Mom found it under the sink. She was looking for oven cleaner. She slammed the bottle on the snack bar and said, "Edward, what is this?"

"Vodka, dear." He smiled sweetly. "For the little people."

Mom frowned. "What little people?"

"These little people," he said in a high-pitched voice. He tapped his finger on the snack bar like he was counting their little heads.

I thought it was funny and giggled. Mom glared at me for a second. Then she went back to glaring at Eddie.

"Didn't we have an agreement about this?"

"It was a gift, dear."

"What idiot would give vodka as a gift to *you?*"

"Someone unenlightened, I'm sure. If you'll look closely at the seal, Lynne, you'll notice it hasn't been broken."

Mom frowned. She twisted the cap, breaking the seal. Then she emptied the bottle down the drain. Even though it looked like water, it had a funny smell. Mom tossed the empty bottle into the trash. "Next time, politely decline gifts like that," she said, and stormed downstairs. A few seconds later, loud angry drums pounded from the basement.

Eddie and I just stood there for a minute. Finally he said in a fake British accent, "I do believe Mummy is miffed."

I knew the situation was serious, but I still laughed. Probably because we had just studied understatement in English class. Besides, Eddie wasn't the bad guy. He had never opened the bottle.

Eddie smiled along with me. "It really was a gift."

I nodded.

"It's impolite to reject gifts. Even from idiots."

I nodded again.

Mom crashed the cymbals downstairs.

"So, Ace," he said slowly. "If some other idiot should happen to give me a bottle like that, where could I put it? You know, so your mom won't find it?"

I thought for a minute. "Back corner of my closet, I guess. Even I don't look back there very often."

He laughed. "Cool. I'll keep that in mind. Thanks."

A week later Mom started going to a group called Al-Anon

on Monday nights. It's kind of an offshoot of Alcoholics Anonymous, except it's a meeting for people who have friends or relatives who are alcoholics. Mom told me that she wasn't going because of her argument with Eddie. She said just seeing the bottle under the sink made her realize she still needed to work things out from having a father and an ex-husband who were alcoholics. She even invited me to go to Alateen, which is like Al-Anon for kids. I told her I didn't need it. I didn't even remember my real dad and we rarely visited my grandparents, so how could I have issues about alcoholics?

I found the new bottle in the back of my closet the day after Mom started Al-Anon. I was looking for ski gloves. The bottle looked just like the one Mom had found. Its seal wasn't broken either. I asked Eddie about it one night when Mom was practicing her drums. He told me to ignore it; it was just another one of those idiotic gifts. I'd ignored it so well I'd forgotten all about it.

Until now.

"Ace?" Eddie prompted. "Hello? That drink?"

I jumped and stared across the desk at Eddie. He held up a ten-dollar bill.

I shuddered on the inside. It was one thing for Eddie to play music behind Mom's back. But drinking?

Eddie gently snapped the bill between his fingers. "Just this once?"

Last night I'd counted my money. I still needed forty-three dollars to afford Silhouette Racing Shoes. My stomach fluttered. I almost told Eddie no. But I was forty-three dollars short. All I'd made at the yard sale was seven bucks. I blinked at the ten in Eddie's hand. He said he only wanted one nip.

How big was a nip? Bigger than a sip but smaller than a gulp? That didn't seem so bad. If that was all he wanted, maybe it would be okay.

I reached for the bill. And the mug.

I walked slowly down the hall to my room. I headed first to my desk and tucked the ten-dollar bill into my bank envelope. That was the easy part. With a nervous sigh I poked my head inside my closet and reached to the back. When I lifted the bottle it felt lighter than the first time I'd held it. Once I brought it into the light I saw why.

The seal was broken. A quarter of the vodka was missing. I felt a twinge in my chest. Did that mean Eddie drank a dozen nips in eight months or a couple of glasses in two days? How much did a person have to drink to be an alcoholic?

"What are you doing in there?" Eddie called out. "Distilling it?"

My shaking hands slopped a gulp's worth of vodka into Eddie's mug. I hurried back to Eddie's study and set the mug on his desk.

"Thank you. I think," he said. He leaned forward and peered into the mug. He sat back and looked at me sharply. "You weren't in there drinking it, were you?"

I made a face at him. "Are you kidding? I looked up vodka in the dictionary once. It's made out of rotten potatoes."

"Not always, but hold onto that thought, Ace," Eddie said. "I don't want *you* getting hooked."

"Same with you," I shot back. Then I cringed, afraid my stepdad would tell me to mind my own business.

He just stared at the mug. "You know," Eddie said, "your mom can't make me stop drinking. It has to come from me." He tapped his chest. "Inside me."

Suddenly I felt trembly. I didn't know why, but he was scaring me.

Eddie folded his hands on top of his desk and focused on the coffee mug again. "I probably won't drink it anyway. Just wanted to look at it. Kind of a test, ya know? A pop quiz. To prove I can resist it." He looked up again. "See? Willpower."

I waited for a silent count of twenty. "Want me to put it back now?" I asked.

He shook his head. "Leave it." He swiveled back to his computer.

I slipped out of the room. If Eddie failed the pop quiz, I didn't want to know.

Chapter Seven

On Thursday, Mom and I ate breakfast alone again. Ever since summer session ended at the college almost three weeks ago, Eddie had been taking advantage of his time off by sleeping late. Well, I didn't miss him. He didn't know it yet, but I wasn't speaking to him.

There was something Mom didn't know, too. For the past two weeks Eddie had been sneaking out to play in Frizzy Guy's band on the nights she went to Al-Anon or paralegal class. I wanted to tell her. Except, I told myself, the truth might hurt Mom more than it would Eddie.

Why couldn't he just tell her himself? "Oh, by the way, Lynnie, I'm playing bass in a cover band. Now that I'm making extra money, you don't have to work so much overtime anymore." But he never did. So I decided to stop speaking to him.

I slapped grape jelly on my toast and took an angry bite. Of course Eddie would never say anything. That would be too honest.

The phone rang and made me jump. That's how focused I was on being disgusted with Eddie.

"If that's Aunt Lucy," Mom said, "tell her I just left."

Geez, now even Mom was telling little white lies. I tried to turn her honest by pointing at my chewing mouth. "Eating," I mumbled.

"Please, sweetie? I have to get to the office early today. You know what happens when Lucy and I start talking."

Still chewing, I answered the wall phone above the snack bar. My greeting sounded more like "whump-o" than hello.

"Wanna make ten bucks?" Domino said from the other end.

I swallowed the rest of my toast fast. "Sure!"

Mom raised her eyebrows in a who-is-it? look. I pointed toward Dom's house. She nodded.

"Can you come over in five minutes?" asked Dom. "We've got a lawn mowing job."

I looked down at my outfit. I had on tattered jeans and one of Eddie's long-sleeved shirts. I'd sneaked it from his closet. All of mine were in the laundry. "Okay," I said.

Mom collected her purse and car keys.

"How hot is it out there?" I asked Dom. I wasn't sure if I should change into shorts.

"Kinda cool. It's supposed to rain later. Tell Eddie to pick us up around noon. We'll be at Eighteen Mill Road." Dom hung up before I could say anything.

Mom headed toward the door that led to the garage.

"Wait!" I called.

She paused.

"Can you tell Eddie to pick up Domino and me at Eighteen Mill Road later? We're mowing lawns today. Please?"

Mom's forehead wrinkled. "You don't need me for that."

Actually I did, since I wasn't speaking to Eddie. I couldn't tell her that, though, or she'd want to know why. I said, "He's your husband and stuff. I can't go in there. He's in bed."

Mom rolled her eyes. "Leave him a note. He never remembers anything you tell him when he's half asleep anyway." She blew me a kiss and shot out the door.

I rarely wrote notes to Eddie. It put me back in the dilemma of what to call him. I used up a few minutes tapping the pen against my jaw and trying to think of a neutral greeting.

Dear Guy Who Married My Mom.

Nope. Too long. I settled for a simple *hi.* Then I jotted my request and taped the note to his coffee mug. That way Eddie would know the message was for him.

I poured a glass of milk. One sip and a horn beeped. I gulped the rest and ran outside.

A shiny blue pickup idled in the Webers' side of the driveway. Dom and his Uncle Vince were loading the last of the lawn mowing equipment into the truck bed.

"Hey, Ace," Domino said. He socked my arm in greeting. "Took you long enough."

I eyed all that equipment. Besides the lawn mower, there were two rakes, a gas can, hedge clippers, and a box of leaf bags.

"Is all that stuff going to fit in Eddie's car?" I asked.

"You'd be surprised," said Dom. "One time I got twice this much in Jason's car."

We piled into the truck. I sat between Vince and Domino as we drove out of town. An old lady named Mrs. Hodge owned the yard we were going to mow.

Rain clouds covered the sun. We passed an old farmhouse, then the paved road narrowed. Bushes and tree limbs crowded toward us.

Domino rolled down his window. Earth and pine smells

filled the truck. A zillion invisible bugs sputtered and hissed from the trees.

Vince's truck rolled to a stop in front of a lopsided stone house. It was partially hidden by fir trees with poor posture. The carport was empty.

"Is anyone home?" asked Vince.

"Mrs. Hodge doesn't drive," Domino said. "Her son takes her places."

Dom hopped out of the truck and strode to the front door to let Mrs. Hodge know we were there. Vince unloaded the equipment and drove away with a wave.

"First, we'll pick up all the loose sticks," Dom said. He pulled two leaf bags out of the box and handed one to me. "Then I'll mow and you trim bushes. When I'm done, we'll both rake." Dom peered up at the cloudy gray sky. "If we're quick, we might even finish before the rain starts."

The backyard was crowded with trees and shrubs. The high-pitched chittering of the bugs sounded louder, too. I gazed at the treetops. They grew so high I got a stiff neck looking up at them. Even though we were in a forest, the clearing behind the house had plenty of grassy space for Domino to mow. There were dozens of shaggy bushes for me to trim. It looked like a lot of work for only ten bucks, but I'd promised Domino. Besides, as small as the pay was, I needed every penny. For the past week I'd been buying so many different colored shoelaces I wasn't sure I'd ever be able to afford the shoes to go with them.

Dom and I worked well together. We filled four leaf bags with pinecones and sticks. Since we only threw a couple of pinecones at each other, we managed to finish that part of the job in record time. Then Domino revved his mower and took off. The mower's happy buzz gave the woods a homey feel. I rolled up my sleeves and started pruning.

The first ten minutes were almost fun. I snipped and snapped at the cowlicks on the bushes. Ten minutes later, the wood handles began to rub my hands. Next my arms started to ache. An hour passed. My palms grew blisters. This was way too much work for just ten bucks. More time groaned by.

A fat raindrop hit my shoulder, followed by another. I smiled at the sky. If it rained hard enough, maybe Eddie would rescue us sooner.

Domino finished the backyard and zoomed to the front. A light, steady rain pattered on the leaves. I tackled the next to last bush with new energy.

I heard Domino cut off the engine. "Lawn's done," he called. "We might as well finish up while we wait for Eddie."

We raked and bagged grass and bush clippings. The rain fell harder, drenching our clothes. Eddie was so late that Mrs. Hodge took pity on us and invited us inside. She looked like a plump little granny with curly white hair and glasses. Her warm house smelled like animal crackers and mildew.

Mrs. Hodge let me use her phone to call Eddie. She led me to her cluttered living room. An old black rotary phone sat on a doily-covered table.

I dialed the number. The phone made a purring sound on the other end. One ring. Two. Three. I counted nine before I finally hung up. Eddie must have forgotten to turn on the answering machine again. But why wasn't he home? He only played in Frizzy Guy's band at night. I stalked back to the kitchen with the bad news.

"Think Jason's home?" I asked. I was furious. How could Eddie forget us?

Domino pinched up his face. He always looked like he'd just tasted a bad pickle when he had to ask his brother for a favor. I crossed my fingers the whole time he dialed the phone. Fortunately, Jason answered. Twenty minutes later, we squeezed all the equipment into the trunk and backseat of Jason's car.

Domino and I climbed into the front, shivering.

"You guys are pathetic," Jason said as he pulled out of Mrs. Hodge's driveway.

"It's not our fault," I said, through chattering teeth. "Eddie was supposed to pick us up."

"Can we have a little heat?" asked Domino.

Jason snorted and passed him his denim jacket. "Take this."

Dom and I huddled close and draped it over our shoulders. The jacket didn't help much since our clothes were so wet. Then, underneath the jacket where nobody could see, Domino slid his hand into mine. I should have been surprised. This was the first time he'd touched me without putting a beetle down my shirt or something. But his hand felt warm and soft. It took my mind off wanting to murder Eddie. All the way home I stared straight ahead, not daring to move.

As soon as we unloaded the equipment, Jason took off in his car. Domino followed me into my garage. As I was about to go into the house he suddenly turned me around and rested his hands on my shoulders. Then he gave me one of those deep-into-the-eyes looks people do in the movies just before they kiss.

For half a second I wondered if I should kiss back if Dom actually tried to kiss me. My insides fluttered. For the first time since I'd known him—and we go back to second grade—I realized that Domino was a guy. Not just any guy. A guy with swimming pool blue eyes and lips that might be fun to kiss.

Domino's face was close to mine. We *were* going to kiss! I hoped our noses wouldn't bump. That would be embarrassing. I leaned in a little more. Through my pounding pulse I heard a car pull into the drive.

A car door banged. Dom jumped back. He stuffed his hands in his pockets.

So much for the kiss.

"Asa!" Eddie said, stomping into the garage. "Where were you?"

"Me?" I cried, forgetting that I had vowed not to speak to him. "Where were *you?*"

"Driving all over the countryside looking for Eighteen Hill Road."

I tried to get a word in, but Eddie wasn't listening. He was too busy telling us the street numbers for Hill Road started at one hundred. He looked for us at One-Eighteen Hill Road. That yard (according to Eddie) was the size of a piccolo case. Next he drove to Hill Top Road. Nothing. Hillendale Avenue was a cul-de-sac. Sunny Hill Road had row homes. The excuses went on and on. The whole time Domino kept his cheeks puffed out to keep from laughing. But it wasn't funny to me. It was stupid.

"Mill Road!" I screamed.

"What?" Eddie looked dumbfounded.

"My note said Eighteen *Mill* Road."

Eddie pulled the note out of his pants pocket. He frowned at it. He even turned it upside down and squinted at it. By now Domino was hugging himself and stamping the floor.

"Does that look like an *M* to you?" Eddie held the paper under Dom's nose.

A big *ha!* exploded from Domino's lips. I held my breath. If I had laughed in Eddie's face he would have quit talking to me for a month. But since Domino was the one who'd laughed, Eddie started laughing right along with him. I snorted in disgust. It was probably a guy thing. The two of them slapped a high five. Then Eddie strolled inside the house, still chuckling.

"He can't help it, Ace," Domino said. "He's a musician. They live in a whole different world."

"Yeah," I said, glaring at the floor. "Right." It wasn't just that Eddie couldn't read my note. His breath smelled like beer. Had Domino noticed? I hoped not. If Domino asked me if I thought Eddie had tried looking for us in a bar, I wouldn't know what to say.

"Well, here's your ten," Domino said, saving me from having to make up some stupid story. He handed me a limp, damp bill. Then he started to lean toward me again.

Eddie poked his head back into the garage.

Dom pulled away a second time.

I clenched my teeth *and* my fists. Why did Eddie have to ruin everything? Now Dom would never kiss me.

"Ace," said Eddie, "let's not tell your mom about this, okay?"

I didn't look at him. I just nodded. He disappeared again.

Domino grinned and jabbed his thumb toward the door Eddie had just closed. "He's worse than a jack-in-the-box."

"Yeah," I muttered.

"Forget it," Dom said. He thumped me in the arm. "Hey, Ace, you're a good worker. Maybe sometime we can work together again. Or something." He turned to go.

"Hey, Dom!" I said. I didn't want him to leave yet. If he stayed one more minute, maybe…

He turned around.

Now that I had his attention, I didn't know what to say. My brain sent the first thing it thought of to my mouth. "You're an okay boss."

Domino grinned. Then he nodded and walked out of the garage.

My heart pounded just thinking about how close we'd stood a minute ago. There was definitely something different about Domino and me now. If I told Claire and Joy I was having romantic thoughts about the goofy guy next door they'd probably laugh in my face.

So I just wouldn't tell them.

Chapter Eight

Day by day, penny by penny, my shoe fund grew bigger. Finally, on Labor Day— the day before school started—I found the last nickel I needed to buy Silhouette Racing Shoes (seventy-nine ninety-five on sale). I dug it out from under a couch cushion. I gripped that nickel in my hand and did a victory dance. I'd earned my Silhouette money without an allowance! I'd even earned it without a baby-sitting job.

My victory dance didn't last long. On that rainy Monday I learned a valuable lesson: Never wait till the day before school starts to buy new shoes if your mom is fighting a late summer cold.

After breakfast, when I slipped into her and Eddie's room to steal Eddie's blue flannel shirt, she was still in bed. The air smelled like the menthol stuff she rubbed around her nose. That's how I knew Mom had lost the summer cold battle.

In the dark room I slid Eddie's shirt over my T-shirt. I stepped up to Mom's shadowy lump in the bed.

"You okay?" I whispered.

"Juice, please?" Mom said in a hoarse voice.

"Sure."

I started to go. She grabbed my hand. "Tiptoe around

Eddie today, honey," she whispered. "I kept him up all night with my coughing, so he'll be overtired."

"Okay." I tried not to sound disappointed. Eddie was my Plan B to get to the mall. But if I played it right, maybe he would take me.

I found Eddie's legs stretched out on the garage floor. The rest of him was hidden under his car. I watched his feet and waited. Quietly.

I was almost eight when Mom married him. In the beginning he mostly ignored me. The longest conversation we had consisted of three sentences. "Hello, Asa," he said. "You get your own room and your own toys. Don't touch my stuff."

For the first year just about all we said to each other was, "Good morning," "Good night," or "Pass the salt, please." But after a while it got better. Eddie even took me to a pony farm for my ninth birthday. That didn't make us best buddies or anything, though. I mean, even now, I felt weird interrupting him while he tinkered under his car. I waited for him to notice me first.

I waited for ages. Nothing. Plan B would have to wait. Fortunately, the mall stayed open till nine P.M. There was still a chance I could get my shoes before tomorrow. I killed time by starting my environmental collage for art class. On the first day of school, Mrs. Valentine, the art teacher, always assigned one.

Rain dribbled down the windows of the family room. I sat on the floor with a dozen of Mom's old magazines spread around me. I didn't find many ecology pictures. These magazines were mostly full of recipes and celebrity gossip. The photos of food gave me the idea to make lunch for Eddie.

Nothing fancy. I just heated up a can of tomato soup and toasted some cheese sandwiches. If I cheered him up with a nice hot lunch he'd have to take me to the mall.

Mom ate tea and toast in bed. Eddie and I sat alone at the table for lunch. Mom was right about Eddie being overtired. He chomped his sandwich in a fog. He didn't even seem to notice that he owed me a favor for cooking.

Eddie looked up and stopped chewing. "I have a shirt just like that." He pointed his spoon at me.

My cheeks burned. If he got mad at me for stealing his clothes, he'd never drive me to the mall.

"Um…is it okay if I borrow this?" I asked.

"As long as you don't spill anything on it."

Eddie went back to chewing. He bobbed his head to an imaginary tune.

My mind flailed about, fishing for an idea to start the please-take-me-to-the-mall conversation. Finally, an idea came to me. I leaped out of my seat and flew to the magazine rack in the family room. I opened the catalog to the earmarked shoe page. I laid the Silhouette Racing Shoe picture next to Eddie's soup bowl.

He studied it in silence.

"Like 'em?" I asked.

"Black running shoes? My feet sweat just looking at them."

"Actually, it's the different laces that make the shoe. I already have most of the colors I need. Today I was supposed to buy the shoes."

Eddie's eyes crinkled up at the corners and his dimple appeared. "Laces first, shoes later. Funny," he said, tapping his temple. "You're very deep, Asa."

That sounded like a compliment. I crossed my fingers and tiptoed into Plan B. "I wondered if...well, if your car's all fixed and everything, maybe you wanted to test drive it to the mall?"

"Okay," he said with a shrug. Just like that. Well, almost. "First, I want to change the oil in your mom's car," he added. "And do a couple of other things. Can you wait till tonight?"

"Sure!" I said quickly. "Thanks."

He went back to the garage. I pounced on the phone by the snack bar and dialed Claire's number. Nobody answered. She was probably at a party. Just about every day was somebody's birthday in her family. Claire had tons of aunts and uncles and cousins.

Even though she hated fads, I called Joy next. I had to share my good news with somebody. "I'm getting my Silhouettes today!" I squealed.

"Asa, Asa, Asa." Her voice sounded tired and disappointed. "You're obviously suffering from delusions."

Joy wants to be a psychologist when she gets older. She practices by analyzing her friends, whether they want her to or not. "You can learn a lot about people by the shoes they wear," she said, "or the shoes they *want* to wear."

Joy didn't believe in popularity. Last year she wrote an article for the school paper about how stupid cliques were. Without meaning to, she became queen of the non-ents. Joy had told me I could be princess of the non-ents if I was interested. I told her no. Even last year I knew I was aiming for something higher. Now the time had come. Shoes were my ticket to popularity.

"I'm getting those shoes," I said over the phone. "I already have nine pairs of laces."

"Nine?" Joy cried out.

"Jennifer Terrell says I need twelve."

"Asa! Jennifer Terrell's group is full of half-witted, superficial blobs of humanity."

"But they'll be wearing really cool shoes this year," I pointed out.

"Forget the shoes. Weave those laces into a pot holder and give it to your mom for her birthday."

"I gotta go now," I said, and hung up. Sometimes Joy was just no fun to talk to.

Mom shuffled out for dinner. Eddie cooked chicken and stir-fried vegetables over rice. Mom ate leftover tomato soup from lunch and went back to bed, leaving us alone.

"Want to go to the mall after I do the dishes?" I asked Eddie.

He nodded. "I'll go see if your mom needs anything before we leave." He walked back to talk to her.

Doing dishes was no easy chore when Eddie cooked. It was like he had a contest with himself to see how many pots and pans he could dirty for one meal. He turned the counters into a sloppy mess. Dishes were piled everywhere. But I worked fast. When Eddie came back, the dishwasher was half loaded. His shoulders looked stiff and he was frowning.

Uh oh. Mom must have said something to put him in a bad mood.

Eddie yanked the basement door open.

My dinner lurched in my stomach. "Um, where are you going?" I called.

He turned and scowled harder. "Africa. What's it look like?"

"But we were going to the mall. You said—"

"You're not ready to go, are you? Look at all that." He pointed at the mess he'd made. "When you're through in here, clean up all that stuff on the floor of the family room."

My mouth stayed open even after Eddie slammed the basement door behind him. That was the first time he'd ever ordered me to do anything. He always let Mom do that.

Sax music seeped upstairs from the basement. It got louder and sounded grumpy. Mom had probably reminded Eddie we were poor again. No wonder he got angry. I knew how it felt to be told you couldn't buy something you really wanted. Sick moms should just sleep and not ruin things.

I jammed the last mixing bowl into the dishwasher and switched it on. Jazz music wailed from the basement. I wiped down the counters. Next I cleaned the family room. By the time all the magazines, including the catalog with the Silhouettes, were back in the rack the music stopped.

The clock over the mantle said it was seven thirty-five. The mall would be open for another hour and a half. There was still time for Eddie to turn happy again and take me to buy my shoes. I folded laundry while I waited. I even hung up Eddie's flannel shirt in his closet without waking Mom.

I let twenty whole minutes pass. He had to be ready by now. I crammed my money in my purse and put on my jacket. I bounded down the steps.

Eddie lay sprawled across the basement couch with his eyes closed. Black headphones were clamped over his ears. He looked like somebody sleeping peacefully. Except for the distinct alcohol smell. Not again! My shoulders drooped. I could never go to the mall with him now.

My energy drained away as I fought back tears. My chest ached with that sinking feeling you get when you run hard but still lose the track meet. Mom told me never to ride in cars with anyone who had been drinking. That meant no shoes for school.

I considered banging Mom's drums really loud to give Eddie a headache. I glared across the room at Mom's cymbals, glistening under the light. Then my gaze fell on Eddie's keyboards and guitars.

He owned a zillion instruments. When Eddie was growing up, Poppy gave him a different one every year for his birthday. Eddie was some kind of musical genius when he was a kid. He was so talented that he toured half of Europe, playing classical piano, before he was twelve. He didn't even go to school. He had a tutor. Mom said that was why Eddie still acted like a kid sometimes. He'd never had the chance to be one.

I stared hard at Eddie. He almost looked like a kid right now with his long lashes and smooth face. But that didn't stop me from hating him. How could I ever turn popular with a drunken stepdad?

I stomped back upstairs. I'd teach Eddie a lesson. I shoved open my closet door and reached for the bottle hidden in the back. He wouldn't pass out anymore if I poured all his vodka down the drain. I grabbed the bottle by the neck and yanked it into the light.

But it was already empty.

Chapter Nine

On the first day of school Mom was still sick in bed. I felt a little queasy myself, but not from the flu. I had the dreaded never-going-to-be-popular-at-this-rate disease. The only antidote was to own Silhouette Racing Shoes.

At breakfast, Eddie, who was responsible for giving me this disease, had the nerve to stare at me with his big blue eyes and say, "I thought we were going to the mall last night."

"You fell asleep," I mumbled.

"Why didn't you wake me?"

I frowned at the cereal flakes turning mushy on my spoon.

Eddie squeezed my shoulder. "I meant to take you, Ace. Honest. Too tired, I guess."

Too drunk is more like it, I thought. I bit my lip to keep from screaming at him.

"I'll take you after work today. How's that?" he said. "Meet me at Fischer Auditorium. My last class is Stage Band rehearsal from three to four-thirty."

I nodded. But it wasn't okay. I needed those shoes now. I couldn't show up on the first day of school in plain old sneakers. All the cool people would be wearing Silhouette Racing Shoes.

On the bus I slumped into my usual seat beside Claire. She had on beige Birkenstocks. Trina, across the aisle, wore clogs. I still felt miserable. All the popular feet that climbed onto the bus sported Silhouette Racing Shoes with orange and brown laces.

At school Joy clapped me on the back. "Good for you, Asa!" She nudged my Nikes with her own pink high-tops. "You took my advice."

I didn't bother to tell her it was Eddie's fault, not her advice, that had kept me out of The Fad. Just then Jennifer Terrell walked by in her shiny Silhouettes. She didn't say anything. She just stared down her nose at my non-ent sneakers. Then she shook her head and kept going. I hoped that didn't mean we weren't secret friends anymore.

At least Jennifer wasn't in my homeroom. Neither was anybody else who wore Silhouettes. I checked everybody's feet. I'd been assigned to a non-ent homeroom. Again.

On the bright side, I got Mr. Evington for eighth grade homeroom and Advanced English. Even though his hair was gray and he wore thick glasses, he didn't act old. In class he bounced around like a kid who'd eaten too much sugar. Some of the guys called him Evelyn because he'd fake crying into his handkerchief whenever he read sad poetry. But he was my favorite teacher. Last year he saved me from detention by giving me a late pass the day Joy tried to be funny by hiding my shoes after gym class.

School let out at noon that day. I figured that a half-day was hardly long enough for anyone to remember what people wore. Maybe nobody would notice when I was a day late joining the fad tomorrow.

Claire and Joy and I hung out around town until three-thirty. Then I said good-bye and rode my bike to Fischer Hall, the music building at Ram's Head College.

I ducked into the auditorium and slid into a back row seat. Eddie stood on stage, conducting a twenty-piece band full of students. They played a snappy, jazzy tune. The music sounded fine to me. But Eddie cut it off with an angry wave of his baton.

"Is anybody watching me?" he shouted. "What do you think I'm doing up here, calisthenics?"

The students bowed their heads a little. I sank down in my chair.

Eddie started the band again. Three bars later he spun toward the saxophone section. "We happen to be in the key of A! If I hear one more G-natural, I'm gonna bang some heads."

He cut the band off two more times. Eddie yelled stuff I didn't think teachers were allowed to yell at students. The students fidgeted in their seats. I crouched lower. He never acted this way at community orchestra. I'd sat in on a few of the professional rehearsals. If anybody played a wrong note in community orchestra, Eddie would clutch his chest and pretend to have a heart attack. Whenever Eddie had to wait for the musicians to find the right music he'd tilt back his head, open his mouth and pretend to swallow his conductor's baton. Sometimes he had fake sword fights with the violin section. Everybody laughed a lot in community orchestra. Everybody also made music that sounded so beautiful it gave me goose bumps.

Halfway through this practice, though, the jazz music lost its snappy feel. Eddie got so angry at all the mistakes that he knocked over his music stand. He stomped off the stage.

I sat in a daze. The stage band looked shocked, too. The guy on first chair trumpet came to life first. He stood up and straightened Eddie's stand. Then he collected the fallen sheet music and quietly took over the rehearsal. I waited a few more minutes. Eddie didn't come back.

Maybe that meant he was done teaching and we could go to the mall now. I slipped out of the auditorium.

But on the way to Eddie's office, my knees started to shake. What if he was still in his temper tantrum mood? The booming pulse in my head said this might not be the best time to mention that ride to the mall. But he was my only hope. Mom was still too sick to drive me. I had to have those Silhouettes and I refused to go one more day without them.

I scuffed to a stop outside Eddie's closed door. I gulped extra air for courage. Then I raised a fist and tapped the door.

"What do you want?" a voice bellowed from inside.

I stumbled backwards. Eddie never yelled like that at home! Before I could run away, he yanked the door open.

"Oh," he said. His mean face morphed into mild surprise. "Asa, come in."

He closed the door behind me and slumped into the chair behind his cluttered desk. I inched to the ugly green vinyl, waiting room–style couch. Three stacks of musical scores covered most of the cushions. I perched on the edge.

A jolt of heat shot through me as Eddie pulled a silver flask out of a bottom drawer. I knew what people kept in silver flasks and it wasn't spring water. He poured the clear liquid into a coffee mug on his desk.

A nervous ripple rolled through me. This wasn't allowed to happen two days in a row! If he put himself to sleep again we'd never get to the mall. Or even home.

Eddie took a long swallow and the lines in his forehead smoothed out. He was switching from his angry mood to a borderline one. This was a crucial period. One wrong word could bring his frown back. And a new frown might mean no trip to the mall for me.

He took another swig. "So-o, Asa, what brings you here?"

A splash of panic hit me. "You told me to."

"Did I? Oh, right," he said with a nod. "The mall."

Even though he'd remembered, I only downgraded my edgy feeling by a notch. I couldn't relax until those Silhouette Racing Shoes were safely on my feet.

"Technically, I'm supposed to be at a stage band rehearsal for another fifteen minutes," Eddie announced.

"Oh," I said, pretending I hadn't seen his tantrum from the back of the room.

"But I guess I could let them off a little early tonight." He poured a second drink from the flask. I felt jittery all over again. Mom's rule about never riding in the car with drinkers played over and over in my head.

"Is it okay to…uh, drink that and drive?" I asked in a quiet voice.

Eddie glared at me. "You want the shoes or not?"

I bowed my head. My cheeks burned, my stomach felt wobbly. Part of me knew I shouldn't go with him. The part with feet demanded those sneakers.

Eddie put down his mug. "Let's go. I'll meet you outside."

In the car I secretly sniffed at the air. He was sucking on a mint. It didn't hide anything. He just smelled like mint and alcohol. Mint and alcohol and aftershave.

My mouth went dry as we passed a speed limit sign. It said thirty-five. Eddie's speedometer wavered toward fifty. He passed a tractor-trailer with barely enough room to move into our lane before a car whizzed by the other way.

"What's the matter with you?" he snarled at me.

I guess I had a bug-eyed look on my face. I swallowed hard and said, "Mom might get mad at me if I'm in a car crash."

She'd get even madder at Eddie. I guess he figured that one out on his own because he said in a soft voice, "It'll be okay, Ace. We won't crash, promise."

The speedometer needle inched back to where it belonged.

A few minutes later he pulled into the parking lot at the mall. The car rolled to a stop at a row of empty spaces. Eddie turned to me with a smile. "See?" he said, sounding happy again. "All in one piece." But his car took up two spaces. I hoped the lady pulling in next to us didn't notice.

"You don't need me, right?" he asked at the front entrance. "You know where I'll be. We'll meet back at the car in…" Eddie checked his watch. "Half an hour?"

I nodded and bolted down the corridor, past the gushing fountain toward the shoe store. The way my luck was going, I had to hurry. I didn't want some other non-ent to get there before me and buy the last pair of Silhouettes.

I spotted my shoes right away. They were on display at the far wall. I rushed toward them, ready to make a sale.

Two feet away I froze. My shoulders drooped. The price tag on the Silhouette shelf said *eighty*-nine ninety-five. This couldn't be happening!

"May I help you?" a man's voice said from behind me.

Usually salespeople ignored me. I glanced around to see if he meant somebody else. We were alone in the shop.

I turned and peered up at him. "I thought—I mean, they

were seventy-nine ninety-five." I pointed at the Silhouette display.

The salesman beamed back. "That was the sale price. Would you like to try a pair?"

"Sale price?"

"Yup. Back-to-school sales are over. Sure you don't want to—"

"No thanks." I stomped out.

They weren't on sale! How could they not be on sale?

I found Eddie at the Musical Box, riffling through the piano CDs in the classical section. He pulled one out and turned it over. I stepped up to him.

"That was quick," he said, scanning the titles on the back.

I scowled hard to keep from crying.

He finally looked at me. "Sold out?"

My eyes wanted to water up. I wouldn't let them. "Not on sale anymore," I said through clenched teeth.

Eddie put the CD back. "How short are you?"

"Ten bucks."

Eddie let out a mint alcohol sigh. "I don't know if I can help. We're on a tight budget these days, Ace."

"Can we try another mall? Please? Maybe they're still on sale somewhere else."

Eddie took me by the elbow. "Show me this shoe store."

I led him straight to the Silhouette shoe display. We were still the only customers in the place.

The salesman bounded up to us like we were brand new customers. "How can I help you folks today?"

"My young colleague would like to try a pair of those black ones," Eddie said, pointing.

The salesman nodded. I gave him my shoe size and he disappeared into the back room.

I shifted my weight from one foot to the other. Was Eddie going to sneak a ten-dollar bill out of his wallet and let me have the shoes after all?

Eddie picked up the sample shoe. His eyes bugged out over the price. "Eighty-nine dollars! Are they kidding? We paid ten for running shoes when I was your age."

"Yeah, but they didn't have holograms back then," I pointed out.

The salesman reappeared with a big black box. The Silhouettes were inside. My eyes widened to take in the shiny black leather and the cool bolt. My foot slid easily into the first shoe. I wiggled my toes, enjoying the cool cushiony inside. I *had* to have these Silhouettes.

"Thought these things were seventy-nine," Eddie said. He sat next to me and turned the display shoe upside down.

"You're thinking of the sale price, sir," the salesman said. He tied the Silhouette shoelaces. "That ended yesterday."

My head shot up. Eddie had to kick in the extra ten now, Mom's budget or not. We both knew he'd slept through the sale.

Eddie thumped his watch. He held it to his ear even though it ran on a battery. "Here's the trouble," he said, slapping it again. "My watch seems to have stopped. I thought this was yesterday."

The salesman laughed. He patted the top of my foot. "How's that?" he asked me.

I stood and walked to the mirror on spongy soles. They felt perfect. They looked perfect. They'd look even better with blue and gold laces. Jennifer had said the next lace combination would be our school colors.

"I'll bet these shoes only cost a dollar to make."

I pivoted toward Eddie. How was he helping things by insulting the clerk?

"This store probably bought them for five," he added. "I'll give you fifty."

I almost choked on my gum. Fifty? Was he crazy?

"I'm sorry, sir," the salesman said. "We don't negotiate prices."

Eddie shrugged. "Maybe you should. How badly do you want to sell us something?"

An explosion of heat went off in my face. Eddie could win some kind of award for embarrassing people. I turned toward the front of the store. Fortunately, nobody from my school walked by.

"They're eighty-nine ninety-five, sir," the salesman said in a calm, take-it-or-leave-it voice.

"How many have you sold today?" asked Eddie. "This place is a tomb. I'll bet I'm your first customer. I'll pay the sale price."

"Sir…"

I wanted to shrink to the size of a shoehorn. If anybody found out my stepdad tried to bargain with a mall salesman for my fad shoes, I'd have to transfer to a new school.

"Do you have a manager hiding in the back somewhere?" asked Eddie.

"No," the salesman said, losing patience.

"Then call him or her on the phone," Eddie said in his no-nonsense voice. "Tell your boss you're on the verge of losing a sale."

Correction. We'd have to move to a new state. Maybe even a whole new country.

The salesman's face turned as red as mine felt. He stormed to the phone at the front counter.

"Let's go," I whispered. I yanked the Silhouettes off my feet with shaking hands. "He won't let us have them."

"Stay cool," Eddie said, full of confidence.

Ten minutes later I collapsed onto the front seat of his car. A big black shoebox, bought at the sale price, fell across my lap.

"Thanks," I said weakly.

"Hey, no prob," Eddie said with a grin. "That was kinda cool, haggling with the guy, wasn't it? It could've gone either way, but we showed him, didn't we, Ace?"

"Uh huh," was all I could say.

So many conflicting thoughts were bouncing off the walls in my head. On the one hand, popular kids never haggled. If they'd been there to see Eddie doing it, I would've been banned from the universe. On the other hand, now that I owned a brand new pair of Silhouette Racing Shoes, I could join The Fad and turn popular.

Maybe Eddie's haggling skills weren't so bad after all. As long as they stayed secret.

Chapter Ten

omino's and my bus stop was in front of our double driveway. I bounced to it the next morning on springy, black soles. Domino gave me his usual punch in the arm. He hadn't acted like he wanted to kiss me again since that day in my garage, so I played along like it had never happened.

I still wasn't used to his new, end-of-summer haircut. His white-blonde hair was so short his ears poked out.

I shook one Silhouetted foot with its blue and gold laces at him. "Say good-bye to the non-ent Asa."

Domino looked sad. "It was nice knowing you, Ace."

"Not that kind of good-bye," I said, grinning. "I'm leaving the outer fringe, not the planet."

Domino shrugged. "If you say so. First they'll tell you how to dress, then they'll tell you who you can hang out with. Your friends can only be from inside the group, you know."

"Then I'll get you inside the group," I said.

"Hey, here's an idea," Dom said, his face brightening. "I can try to get *you* into *my* group."

"Sure," I said. Domino's group was pretty much made up of a bunch of weird guys who liked to make armpit noises in music class.

"And we don't make people wear only one kind of shoe," Dom added.

I nodded. "Thanks," I said, hoping I hadn't made him feel bad.

Domino nodded back. A second later his face turned serious. It had that same look the time we almost kissed in my garage. My heart skipped eagerly. I leaned toward him. The school bus rumbled up and the doors opened with a hiss.

Domino socked me in the arm and leaped onto the bus ahead of me. He bounced down next to Buddy Myers. I went back to pretending we hadn't almost kissed again and sat beside Claire. I rested my right foot on my left knee and wiggled my shoe to make sure she saw it.

Her eyes widened. "You got them!" She bent over for a closer look. "They're even better in person." She poked at my holographic lightning bolt.

"Plus, they're amazingly comfortable," I said.

I settled back. Life couldn't get any sweeter.

At the next bus stop Claire gazed out the window. "That's weird," she said, nose against the windowpane.

A line of kids was waiting to board the bus. Rachel and Hilary were second in command in Jennifer Terrell's group. The two of them were easy to spot. They always dressed like twins. Only popular girls could get away with something that babyish. Today they wore matching green plaid skirts and green ribbons in their sweet-corn yellow hair. Yesterday they'd worn brown and orange laces like everybody else in The Fad. But today they were Silhouette-less.

"Maybe they forgot." I sat back again. Or maybe they weren't popular enough to know today was blue and gold laces day.

"Maybe," Claire said in a doubtful voice.

I didn't start worrying until after a few more stops. None of the other popular kids who got on our bus were wearing Silhouettes either. By the time we pulled up to Wollerton Middle School, I had to face the awful truth: I was the only person wearing black leather racing shoes with blue and gold laces.

I stayed in my seat after everybody else piled off the bus.

"I can't go in," I whispered to Claire.

"You have to," she whispered back.

I shook my head. "Ms. Maxwell can give me a ride back home. I'll say I'm sick."

It wasn't a lie. My head was swirling the way it did when I started down the steepest hill on a roller coaster. Plus, my stomach wasn't sure if it wanted to keep my breakfast or not.

"Let's go, girls," said Ms. Maxwell, our bus driver.

My legs felt too wobbly to stand on their own. Claire helped me up.

"It won't be that bad," said Claire. "I mean, how many people look at your feet on an average day?"

"I hope nobody," I mumbled.

The lobby was crowded as usual. Kids laughed and jostled each other. Everybody turned dead quiet when I started walking down the hall. I felt the painful jab of a zillion eyeballs, all gawking at my holographic lightning bolt.

They say you can't die from humiliation. My life flashed in front of my eyes anyway. I almost fainted.

"They're staring," I whispered to Claire.

"Not at you. The principal probably just walked by and that shut everybody up," Claire said, but I didn't believe her.

She walked with me to my locker. That's when I saw it,

scribbled across the front of my locker in red magic marker: OTWCW. There it was in bold letters, proof that everybody *had* noticed.

I pulled away from Claire and flew down the hall to the girls' room. Claire called to me but I didn't stop. I burst through the swinging door. A gang of stuck-ups stood by the mirrors, putting on makeup. They practically dropped their lip-glosses into the sink so they could fall over themselves laughing at me.

I zoomed past them and locked myself in the last stall. Hiding didn't help. I heard giggling. Someone even said, "We see your feet! We see your feet!"

I stood on the toilet seat. That only made them laugh harder. I closed my eyes and waited for the first bell. Finally, it rang. The girls cleared out, still laughing.

Now that I was alone I could breathe again. But before I could climb down, I heard the door open one more time.

"Asa?" It was Jennifer Terrell.

I froze, crouched on top of the toilet. I clenched my eyes shut. I pretended to be invisible.

"Asa, I know you're here. I saw you come in."

A fat tear slipped through my eyelid. It rolled down my hot face.

"I'm sorry about the mix-up, Asa, it was probably my fault," Jennifer said in one breath. "When I said we'd be wearing school colors, I didn't mean today. I meant at the pep rally next Friday. Everybody knows you can't wear Silhouettes every day. I mean, they don't go with every outfit, right?"

I buried my face in my arms.

"They're just shoes, Asa," Jennifer said softly. "Okay?"

I didn't answer. I couldn't.

Half a minute later I heard the door swing open and shut. She was gone.

The late bell sounded. I don't know why I had thought I could escape in here. I had learned this lesson years ago: never hide in the bathroom. There was always somebody coming in to comb her hair or tug at her tights. Lady teachers poked their heads in from time to time to check for hiders, too.

I splashed cold water over my face. All the other kids were in their classes now. The hallway was deserted. That's when I decided to leave school. Nobody would notice. Unfortunately, I hadn't ridden my bike today. It was an easy ride home but a long way to walk. That left only one option. I had to call a parent.

There was a pay phone in the main lobby. To reach it I had to pass the principal's office. His door was open. I whooshed by. Nobody called out. No roaming teachers caught me either. The lobby was as empty as the halls.

At the phone I dug through my purse for change and punched in Mom's office number. The phone rang. I cringed. Mom was sure to tell me this was what happened to kids who followed the masses instead of being their own person.

The receptionist at the law office answered the phone. I almost hung up. I didn't want a big lecture from Mom. All I wanted was a ride home.

I took a deep breath and asked for my mom, but the receptionist told me I'd just missed her. She'd gone to the courthouse to file some papers. Did I want to leave a message?

I shook my head, even though the receptionist couldn't see me. "No thanks," I said. "I'll talk to her tonight."

I hung up. That left one other person. Eddie.

After yesterday I wasn't sure I wanted his help again. He was the only person I knew who could embarrass me by doing something simple, like buying shoes. Still, he had a car that could drive me away from this terrible place.

I fumbled through the loose papers in my knapsack for the emergency card with Eddie's work number on it. I dropped my last quarters into the phone slot. My finger thumped in the number for the college music department. An embarrassing stepfather couldn't be much worse than a mom who followed her own drumbeat.

Eddie wasn't in his office either. The secretary said he was in class. This time I left a message for him to pick me up at school. *Soon.*

I knew it was a long shot, but I plodded to the nurse's office and asked to go home.

She raised her eyebrows. "I can't just let you leave, young lady. That is not school policy."

"But I'm sick." To prove it I started blubbering. "I already called my uh, stepdad. He's coming for me."

The nurse just looked at me for a minute. Since Eddie was already on the way—I hoped—she put me to bed.

I lay on the little cot with a damp cloth on my forehead. Rubbing alcohol and Band-Aid smells from the cabinet wafted around me. I heard some kid come in with a bloody nose. After that it turned quiet. Quiet enough to take a nap, which I did. A little after ten-thirty, familiar footsteps and jingling keys entered the nurse's office.

Eddie's voice said, "Is Asa Philips in here?"

I yanked the cloth off my head and sat up.

"Are you a guardian?" asked the nurse.

I hurried out of the little room before he could answer. He wrapped his arm around me just like a real dad.

"Here she is," Eddie said. He signed a paper for the nurse and guided me out.

"What's wrong?" he asked me in the parking lot. "Headache, stomachache?"

"Everything." I gulped more air to keep from crying in front of him.

"Do you need a doctor?"

"No."

"Your mom?"

"No! I'll be okay in a minute."

I slumped into the passenger seat. Before he started the car, Eddie leaned over and pressed his hand against my forehead. Mom did the same thing to see if I had a fever. I felt better right away. His breath smelled like a grape lollipop today. He always took one from the basket at the teller window when he went to the bank. "No fever," Eddie said. He straightened up. "Where am I taking you?"

"Can't I just stay with you? I don't think I want to be alone right now."

He shrugged and started the car. "It'll be boring, but okay." He turned the car toward Ram's Head College.

At his office, Eddie cleared the music scores off his couch for me. He sat on the edge of his desk, facing me. "Is this one of those, uh…monthly problems?"

I gaped at him. Eddie wasn't supposed to ask questions about monthly problems. He was a guy. He wasn't even allowed to *know* about monthly problems. Only Mom knew about stuff like that. If she was telling him our secrets I'd never speak to her again.

"No!" I said in my blackest voice, and hoped he'd get the hint to change the subject. I bounced onto the couch and crossed my legs, yoga style.

Eddie raised an eyebrow. "Do you have that disease kids get when they haven't studied for a test?"

Now I frowned even harder. Didn't he know *anything?* "Whoever heard of having a test on the second day of school?" I snapped.

He rubbed a hand over his face. "Then what is it?"

I took a deep breath. Okay, maybe he meant well. I bowed my head, trying to think of a way to explain it. But how could Eddie understand? Nobody laughed at musical geniuses. They laughed at non-ents.

A big achy blob pulsed in my throat. My neck always knew when I was going to cry before the rest of me did. I swallowed a couple times to make it go away.

"Ace?" he said softly. "Are you going to tell me?"

"It's these," I said in a choked voice, pointing at my shoes. I squinted through watery eyes at my feet. I despised those colored laces and black leather. I yanked off my Silhouettes and hurled them across the room. They clanged against Eddie's metal wastebasket and bounced onto the tile floor.

"Whoa," Eddie said, raising his hands in surrender. "Is this some kind of protest thing?"

I drew my knees to my chin. Then I buried my face in my arms and sobbed.

"Ace, it's okay," Eddie said. "Don't cry, all right?"

I knew by his nervous voice he was scared. He probably wasn't used to hysterical stepdaughters bawling in his office.

"I'll get you a soda," he said. "You want a soda?"

I flopped face-down on the couch and cried even harder.

"Asa, please don't do this." He knelt beside the couch and patted my shoulder. "Time to stop now, okay? Let's sit up."

Eddie helped me up. He sat next to me with his arm around my shoulders.

"That's better, isn't it?" He offered me his handkerchief.

It had to be better, even if it wasn't. Eddie looked like he was about to panic and call my mom.

I sniffed and dabbed at my eyes.

"I'm okay now," I lied. More tears wanted to pour out. I held them back.

"We'll just sit here and relax for a minute," Eddie said.

I snuggled close to him, trying to calm down. If only my mind would quit remembering those ugly initials scribbled on my locker, OTWCW.

I shuddered. Eddie hugged me tighter.

"We're all right, Ace, honest."

I knew it was wishful thinking by the desperate way he said it.

"Bet you never did anything so embarrassing you almost died from it." I sniffled.

"Are you kidding?" Eddie snorted. "I'm the former Mr. Music, remember? That costume alone was enough to mortify half my life away."

I almost smiled. The picture with that funny costume still sat on his desk at home. I remembered when he gave it to Mom. A couple of months after her divorce went through she took me to the mall where Mr. Music was signing autographs. Eddie recognized Mom right off. He couldn't talk in public. Instead of a regular autograph he wrote across his picture, "Yes, it's me. I get off at six. Love, Ed."

Mom and I hung around the mall till six so we could go

to dinner with him. The wait was extremely boring for me. So was the dinner. I was only about five at the time.

They didn't fall in love and get married right away. About a week after the autograph session he left the TV show. Mom didn't hear from him for a long time. Then he sent her a postcard saying he was back in the area, teaching music at the college. He also wrote, if she were free, could he meet her for lunch? *That's* when they fell in love.

It wasn't until right now, with Eddie hugging me, that I decided I almost loved him too. I was thinking about asking if I could call him Dad, when he pulled his arm away to check his watch.

"Sorry to comfort and run, Ace," he said, standing up. "I'm late for theory class. Will you be okay here?"

I nodded. Maybe we weren't ready for that dad stuff after all.

Chapter Eleven

I locked myself in my room after dinner so I could be alone in my fad blunder misery. Pretending to be fine at the table so Mom wouldn't suspect anything had worn me out.

Even my pillow couldn't block out the sound of Mom's drums and Eddie's electric guitar blasting from the basement. Eddie had talked Mom into letting him use his electric instruments again. He told her Poppy sent a check to help pay the electric bill. I knew the extra money came from Eddie's secret job. I didn't tell Mom. She sounded so happy to be able to play loud music with Eddie again.

Mom and Eddie liked jamming together. It always made them laugh. Tonight they har-harred all over the place. I was glad they were getting along so well, but their happy voices made me feel more miserable. How could they have fun when my whole world was crumbling?

Downstairs I heard Eddie say, "Move those little feet, babe."

That reminded me of Eddie's little people.

I sat up in bed. His little people hid inside the bottle in my closet. Drinking with them cheered Eddie up sometimes. It also put him to sleep.

Ever since I was six, Mom had been drumming into my head how bad alcohol was for people. She still tells me horror stories about growing up with her alcoholic dad. When Grandpa drank it was like Russian roulette. You didn't know if he'd laugh and tell jokes or if he'd turn violent and smash glasses against the wall.

Anybody with half a brain, Mom liked to say, knew The Bottle was bad news.

But Eddie's bottle was for the little people. And right now I was feeling little enough to slither right under my closed door.

Mom and Eddie wouldn't be coming upstairs to check on me any time soon. Even so, I tiptoed to my closet. As I eased the door open, my heart ricocheted inside my chest. Guilt said: Leave it alone. Desperation said: But what about the little people? If I took just a little-person-sized sip, would that be okay? Or would it turn me into an alcoholic like my grandpa?

I imagined all those little people, laughing and dancing and taking swallows from the bottle. It seemed like a fun party, one that might erase away my OTWCW memories.

I reached way into the back of my closet. The neck of the bottle felt cool to the touch. It also felt heavy. I pulled the bottle into the light as the sound of Mom's drums rat-a-tat-tatted downstairs.

Eddie must have replaced the empty one. The seal wasn't even broken.

Everybody knows you can't sneak a drink from an unopened bottle. I gazed at it till my eyes stopped focusing. Would Eddie remember it was brand new? Should I twist open the cap? The answer *no!* shuddered through me. I quickly hid the bottle again. I didn't want to drink with the little people after all. Besides, I hated the smell of alcohol. And if it smelled bad it probably tasted even worse. Those little people must be crazy.

A loud thud sounded across the room. I jumped and slammed my closet door shut. Then I heard a second thump coming from my window.

I spun around. Through the window above my desk, I spotted Joy. She stood pressed against the pane, making fish faces at me.

Joy almost never used the door when she visited. That was because I lived in a ranch house. Joy liked to lean her fifteen-speed bike against my outside wall. Then she stood on the seat and flattened herself, Spiderman-style, against the glass till I let her in.

I didn't want company tonight. But I didn't want to leave Joy outside like that either. I went over to the window and opened it.

Her backpack plopped onto my desk first. Then Joy bounded into the room. She opened the pack and pulled out my math, geography, and English books.

I groaned as the sight of those books brought back another gut-twisting memory of school and my major humiliation.

"So where'd you go this morning anyway?" Joy asked.

"Eddie picked me up."

"How come? Dentist appointment?"

I frowned. "Funny. Come on, you were there. You saw what happened. I was...you know, whatever that thing is that sounds like ostriches and means everybody hates the sight of you?"

Joy nodded. "Ostracized. Except that isn't exactly what happened. Anyway, I brought your homework."

Homework? Why bother? "I can't go back to school after today," I said. The idea of facing the popular kids again was too horrible to think about.

"Sure you can go back," Joy said.

I flopped backwards onto my bed and squinted at the ceiling so I wouldn't cry again. "I'm OTWCW, remember?"

"You're not out of touch with any world, Ace."

I snorted. That was easy for *her* to say. Nobody wrote OTWCW on her locker.

Joy dove onto the bed next to me. We listened to Mom and Eddie playing rock music downstairs.

"You did one of those Icarus things," Joy said. "Tried to fly too close to the sun and your wings melted."

I frowned, not in the mood to think about Greek mythology. We'd studied Icarus in Ms. Jackson's class last year. "Do you see any waxy feathers on me? I didn't fly. I wore the right laces on the wrong day. That makes me OTWCW forever."

"Here's the thing," Joy said. "There's more to the *real* world than what goes on with Jennifer Terrill's clones." She cocked her head, listening to the music downstairs. "You know, your parents sound good enough to play professionally."

I rolled away from her. I didn't want to think about parents right now. I didn't want to think about anything.

"So…are you coming to school tomorrow, or what?" asked Joy.

I rolled back. "I'm joining the circus."

Joy thought that over. "Well, don't be a clown, okay? You're not funny enough. You could be a magician or a sword swallower."

"If I'm not funny, how come everybody laughed at me today?"

"You're exaggerating again," said Joy.

"So okay, what *did* people say after I left?" I held my breath, convinced it was going to be brutal.

"After you left," Joy announced, "Evington gave us an essay to write in class. He said it was because we're all geniuses in there so we could handle it."

I frowned, not interested in essays. "But what about *me?*"

Joy shrugged. "Most kids were complaining about Evington harassing us on the second day of school."

"Oh," I said, not sure if that was the truth or a lie. "Well, I still don't want to go back."

Joy flipped onto her stomach and propped herself on her elbows. "Okay, the first hour or two will be the hardest. Maybe a few kids will stare. But they'll get tired of it. If you act like you don't care, things will go back to normal by sixth period."

There was a lull in the basement concert. Joy rolled off the bed. She picked up the black shoebox with my Silhouettes inside. I'd left it on the floor by the closet.

"What happens to these?" she asked.

I sat up and shrugged. "I'm thinking about burying them in the backyard. I'll tell Mom they got stolen in gym class. Maybe then she'll get me something else."

Joy dropped the box on the floor. "What a waste."

"I thought you never wanted me to buy them in the first place," I said.

"Well, that was before you became a hero to the outer fringe," Joy said.

"Really?" I asked.

Joy nodded. "They liked it that you made fun of the stuck-ups by wearing their laces. They think you did it on purpose."

"You're kidding." I started to feel better for the first time that day.

Joy grinned. "I may have helped that rumor along a little. I said you were making a statement about how dumb fads are."

That sounded good. Except for one thing. "So if I did it on purpose, how come I left school early?" I asked.

"Death in the family," she replied casually.

I know I've said it before. But Joy's the best liar I know.

I smiled back. "Okay. Maybe I will see you in school tomorrow, then."

"Good. Pick a weird lace combination this time. Like orange and purple."

I stopped smiling. "No way. I'm not wearing those things tomorrow."

"You have to," Joy said firmly. "Wear the Silhouettes every day with clashing laces. It'll make The Fad look so stupid it'll fall apart."

"I can't do that to Jennifer," I said, shaking my head. "She invited me to join in the first place."

Joy raised an eyebrow at me. "If you say so," she said finally. "But that doesn't sound like Jennifer to me. I mean, she mostly hangs out with snobs. And no offense to your parents, but they aren't rich enough for you to be a snob."

"Jennifer likes other people besides snobs," I said.

Joy shrugged. "I still think you should blow The Fad out of the water. At least think about it, okay?" She jumped back out the window. "See ya tomorrow."

After she left I picked up my Silhouette box and pulled out one of the shoes. I poked lightly at the holographic lightning bolt. I had to admit, I still liked the flashy way they looked.

Did I dare wear them again tomorrow?

Nope. The kids from the outer fringe would have to find another hero. I wasn't going to make fun of Jennifer's fad. I threw open my closet door and peered inside again. I owned lots of clothes. All I needed was an outfit that went with a pair of my other shoes. Even Jennifer said Silhouettes didn't go with every outfit.

My eyes zoomed in on my short navy pleated skirt and a pale blue blouse. If I got dressed up, no one would expect me to wear racing shoes. I pulled out the skirt and blouse and draped them across the back of my desk chair for the next day.

At breakfast Mom and Eddie didn't notice I only nibbled at one piece of toast. They chatted merrily to each other. They didn't have a clue what horrors I was about to face at school today.

I also didn't mention to Mom that I'd left school early yesterday. I guess Eddie didn't tell either. When Mom finally looked at me she said, "Asa, why aren't you wearing your new shoes?"

"They'd clash with my outfit," I said.

That seemed to make perfect sense to Mom. She went back to telling Eddie about some boring case at work. I slung my pack over my shoulder and trudged out the door.

At the bus stop Domino stood whistling to himself. He stopped when he saw me. "Hey," he said with a half smile. His eyes glimpsed my feet. "I talked to Brett, by the way. There's an initiation to get in our group, but it's no big deal. All you have to do is put a cat in the teachers' lounge. Neil has one you can borrow."

"Oh," was all I could say. On the one hand I was relieved Dom wasn't holding the Silhouette episode against me. On the other hand, Dom's group was pretty near the bottom of the popularity scale. Did I really want to be in his group, especially when it involved shoving cats into teachers' lounges?

"Uh, I think I'm allergic to cats," I lied.

Dom stepped closer. "For real? Try this. Sniff my shirt."

"What?" I squealed.

"I've been feeding Mrs. Rowan's cats while she's away," Dom explained. "When I go over there in the morning those cats are all over me. If you sniff my shirt and don't sneeze, then we'll know you're not allergic."

Dom moved even closer. We stood almost nose to nose.

"Here," he offered, holding up his sleeve.

I looked into his eyes, so clear and expectant. How could I politely refuse to smell his shirt? How could I tell him I didn't want to join his group without hurting his feelings? If only I could wrinkle my nose and force out a sneeze.

In the end I did the only thing I could think of to take his mind off the cats. I took a deep breath, bent toward him, and kissed him. Right on the lips.

For a second the whole world disappeared. It was just Domino, me, soft lips, and the vague taste of toothpaste. After a minute we eased apart. The world came back. But it didn't seem like the same one. Even Domino looked different.

"Wow," he said. "I've wanted to do that for a month."

"Then why didn't you?" I asked.

"I don't know." Dom shrugged. "You might've kicked me in the shins."

"Maybe," I said, grinning.

Dom looked away. "There's just one complication," he

said. "If you, uh, join my group we'll probably have to pretend that never happened."

I didn't ask why. For now it didn't matter. Domino and I had kissed! I'd wondered how it might feel. Now I knew.

The bus rounded the corner and came to a stop. Dom skipped and I half floated to the bus. We gave each other knowing smiles and sat with our friends. Dom with Buddy Myers and me with Claire.

If anybody looked at my feet on the bus I didn't notice.

At school I know a few stuck-ups whispered behind my back. A lot of eyes zoomed in on my feet. But I didn't care. There wasn't much anybody could say about plain black shoes. Besides, I still had the memory of Domino's kiss on my lips.

The day went faster than I expected. We had pizza for lunch. Nobody threw any at me. I got an A on a pop geography quiz. A fire drill broke up a boring lecture about binary numbers in math class. By sixth period, just as Joy had promised, everybody went back to ignoring me as usual. For once I was happy to be a non-ent.

After final period I found a note inside my locker. Somebody must have slipped it through one of those fish gill vents in the door. It read, "Meet me at the Ram's Head Library at 4:30. I'll be in fiction, the *W* aisle." It was signed simply, *"J."*

I had hoped it would be from Domino, but the *"J"* ruled him out. Besides, Dom had a chess club meeting after school. Joy loved stuffing notes in my locker, but I knew her scratchy handwriting. These letters looked too frilly. Even the *i*'s were dotted with hearts. Joy would never do that.

If Joy hadn't left me the note, then who had? Jennifer Terrell? But why would she want to meet me at the town library? You weren't even supposed to talk in there.

There was only one way to find out.

At home after school I told Eddie I had research to do. I changed into jeans and rode my bike uptown to the library. If it turned out to be a hoax, I figured I could simply take out a book and go home. I just hoped there wouldn't be an army of popular kids waiting to play some humiliating trick on me.

At exactly four-thirty I stood outside the library door. I took a deep breath for courage and entered the building. I inched toward the *W* fiction section. Then I peeked around the stacks and down the aisle.

Jennifer Terrell stood by herself. She held an open book in her hands. So Jennifer *was* the *J!* I was sure she would never send me to a library to make fun of me. She was the one who'd tried to help me be popular.

Jennifer looked up. I smiled and took a step toward her. She frowned and shook her head. I froze, confused.

Jennifer clapped the book shut and marched toward me, eyes straight ahead. She pushed the book into my hands. "Inside cover," she whispered, and strode away.

The book was called *The Friendly Persuasion*, by Jessamyn West. Jammed under the front cover was a sheet of paper. I unfolded it and my eyes bugged out.

Jennifer had given me a list of all the Silhouette days *and* the color combinations for the laces. The list went all the way up to black and orange for the Friday before Halloween. At the bottom of the list Jennifer had written: *I'll pretend I don't know how you got this. Play along. P.S.—The colors can change anytime, but I'll try to keep you updated.* The next Silhouette day was a week from Friday. The popular kids would be wearing blue and gold laces for the pep rally, just like Jennifer had told me before school started.

I stood alone in the *W* aisle and sagged against the stacks in relief. I had the whole secret list! Jennifer had come through for me after all!

This time I'd be more careful about The Fad. I'd keep all my laces and a backup pair of shoes in my pack. If the rules changed unexpectedly, I'd be able to see it from the window of the school bus. With my secret plan I could change shoes or laces before the bus even pulled into the school parking lot. Problem solved. I was back in The Fad!

Now everything would be perfect.

Chapter Twelve

For a whole week nobody wore Silhouette shoes to school. I looked like a regular non-ent. Claire and Joy thought I'd forgotten about The Fad.

But on Friday, the day of the pep rally, I slipped my feet into my Silhouette Racing Shoes and bounded to the kitchen. Mom and Eddie both complimented my blue and gold laces.

At the bus stop I expected a smile and a punch from Domino. Every day since our kiss he'd grinned and socked me in the arm in greeting. I assumed that was our secret code to ward off any teasing. I played along. Today Dom took one look at my holographic lightning bolts and his eyebrows disappeared under his bangs.

"You're wearing those dumb things again?" he said.

I frowned. "Why wouldn't I be? Everybody's wearing them for the pep rally today."

Dom cleared his throat. "Excuse me, but not everybody's wearing them. For instance, *I'm* not."

I stared at the hiking boots on his feet. I still hadn't thrown a cat into the teachers' lounge to join Dom's group. I didn't want him to get started on that, either. I couldn't even kiss him to shut him up this time. "These shoes happen to be extremely comfortable," I said. "It's like walking on clouds."

Domino looked skeptical. "Well you know who walks on clouds," he said.

I just blinked at him. He'd give the punch line whether I wanted it or not.

"Airheads."

This time I socked Domino in the arm. And I didn't mean it as a secret code.

When the bus pulled up I clomped down the aisle. My Silhouettes didn't feel quite as cushiony now. I dropped into the seat beside Claire.

She stared at me. "You have got to be kidding," she said.

"What?" I said innocently.

"Your feet! How can you do this after what happened last time?"

I shrugged, willing to ignore her grumpy attitude. "No, this is different," I said. "I've got it covered this time."

I patted the bulge in my pack where my Hushpuppies hid. I'd change into them in a flash if nobody at the other bus stops was wearing Silhouettes today. "Do you mind if we switch seats? I need to look out the window."

"What for?" Claire huffed. "So you can wave your feet at people driving by? You're not one of them," she added in a low voice. "You realize that, don't you?"

I clenched my fists around the straps on my pack. Best friends were supposed to be happy for each other. Especially when those friends were back on track with their Turning Popular Project.

"Look, just switch with me, okay?" I asked.

Claire just muttered something in reply. But she stood up while the bus was moving so I could wiggle across the seat to the window.

"Let's stay in our seats," Ms. Maxwell said. She glared at us through the rearview mirror.

Claire's nose turned bright pink. That always happened when she got embarrassed.

"Thanks," she said to me.

"You're not welcome," I shot back.

What kind of pep rally day was this going to be with all my friends turning against me? It was making me feel very un-peppy. When I turned popular they'd be sorry.

At the first popular bus stop, I pressed my nose to the window. My eyes zoomed in on all the Silhouette Racing Shoes. Blue and gold laces stood out against the black leather.

I smiled to myself. I didn't have to change shoes after all. Jennifer's list had been right. She hadn't let me down!

Joy rode a different bus so she met Claire and me at our lockers. Joy glanced at my feet and pretended to bang her head against her locker door. "Ace," she sighed. "I thought we cured you of this unhealthy impulse to follow the crowd."

I hated it when her psychology lectures sounded like my mother.

"It could just be a coincidence," I snapped.

Joy rolled her eyes. "Yeah, right," she said. She and Claire took off for class without me.

I slumped against my locker door. Three of my friends had deserted me within twenty minutes. I sure hoped Jennifer's friends would be nicer.

Just as that thought rolled into my mind, Rachel and Hilary appeared. They were dressed in washed-out jeans and fuzzy sweaters. One pink and one blue. The two of them actually blocked my way so they could stare down their noses at me. Not a very friendly greeting.

Chapter Twelve

"What's this?" Hilary demanded. She kicked the tip of my right Silhouette Racing Shoe with hers.

I was only two inches shorter than Hilary and Rachel, but I felt kindergartner-sized standing with them. This wasn't how The Fad was supposed to work. We were all supposed to be instant friends. I didn't want them to think they scared me or anything, so I gave them my best snooty stare.

"I'm just participating in The Fad," I said.

Rachel stepped closer. "It was a lucky guess," she said. "Even a stopped clock is right twice a day."

"Hey, what's up, guys?" Jennifer asked. She slid in smoothly next to Hilary and Rachel. She focused on my shoes. "Oh."

"Oh?" Hilary and Rachel repeated. They were like two angry Barbie dolls. "That's *it?*" Hilary added on her own.

"She isn't in The Fad," Rachel said.

Jennifer just shrugged. "She's wearing the right laces."

Hilary shoved her face so close to mine I smelled her strawberry flavored lip-gloss. "Who told you? That motor-mouth Lindsay Eckert?"

Jennifer stepped between us. "Hil, it doesn't matter," she said. "Anybody who knows the colors is in The Fad. That's the rule. Maybe she has a friend who told her." She gave me a quick side-glance. I knew what that meant. Keep my mouth shut.

"Well, it's been fun chatting," I said, "but I don't want to be late for class. See you guys at the pep rally."

Hilary and Rachel didn't say a word. They pivoted on their Silhouettes and marched down the hall. Jennifer followed them. But she turned for a split second and gave me a tiny smile.

I'd won! Thanks to Jennifer. I smiled all the way to advanced English class.

Mr. Evington was in prime form. "I've been thinking about our first official writing project for the year," he announced in his high-pitched nasal voice. "Are we feeling poetic?"

All the kids in the class groaned. Mr. Evington grinned, showing off the gap between his two front teeth. "Perhaps we're in the mood for a little prose instead, then?"

This time everybody grumbled except Claire. She sat across the aisle on my right. I looked over at her. She was reading a miniature paperback. The book was called *How to Attract the Guy of Your Dreams in Ten Easy Steps.*

I whispered across the aisle, "Is it any good?"

If she was speaking to me, she'd answer.

Claire looked up. I held my breath.

"It makes some good points," she whispered back.

I smiled, relieved. We were still friends.

"I promise not to make you write about your summer vacation," said Mr. Evington. "I want something more creative. How about a short story?"

The groaning started up again, especially after he said the rough draft was due Monday. Who wanted to write short stories over the weekend?

Claire ignored all the protests. She was too busy learning how to attract guys in ten steps or less.

"People," said Mr. Evington, quieting everybody down. "This is *Advanced* English. We do advanced things in here."

More moans came from the class. Claire just smiled and turned a page.

"Does it say anything about how to get rid of freckles?" I asked.

Chapter Twelve

The eighty-seven dots on my cheeks and nose (I counted once) made me look like a little kid. I wanted to look sophisticated, like Jennifer.

"Ms. Philips," Mr. Evington said in a sweet tone. "Did you have a query?"

I sat up straight in my chair. My holographic lightning bolt couldn't save me now. I could feel all eighty-seven freckles pale.

"I was wondering if we could...you know, write out the assignment...like, for people who don't have a computer at home?"

It was a complete lie, but Mr. Evington didn't have to know that.

Joy, who sat behind me, gave me a congratulatory nudge with the end of her pen. She had tutored me on lying a few times in study hall. A warm glow of satisfaction pulsed through me. Not only had I passed one of Joy's learn-to-lie assignments, we were still friends enough for her to tap me with her pen.

"Oh, you don't have one at home?" asked Mr. Evington, sounding concerned.

"Uh, it's...broken," I blurted.

"Well if your computer is out of commission, I'm sure you can use one at the public library after school hours. Otherwise, please feel free to compose in the computer lab here at school. I want these typed. Any other questions?"

Two girls up front were going camping over the weekend. They pleaded with the teacher to extend the deadline until Wednesday. Mr. Evington said no. While they were whining and protesting I let myself relax. He wouldn't be looking my way for a while.

Across the aisle Claire held up her notebook. NO FRECKLE TIPS. EYEBROW PLUCKING?

I shook my head. My eyebrows were one of the few features I liked about my face. Not too thick, not too thin.

Claire flipped the page. Her second note said, TOPICS FOR DATES? HAIR STYLES? BODY LANGUAGE?

I scribbled SHORT STORY TOPICS? in my notebook and held it up.

"Ladies," Mr. Evington said. He eyed us through his oversized glasses. "This is not the Western Union. Kindly refrain from exchanging telegrams."

When Mr. Evington turned to write short story prompts on the blackboard, I held up my notebook to Claire one more time. I had written, I'M PERFECT JUST THE WAY I AM, HA HA.

English class was almost over when Claire smiled and held up her final note: EVEN WITHOUT THE SHOES.

I slumped against the back of my chair. I guess that was supposed to be a compliment, but it still stabbed at me. How could my own best friend not get what I was trying to do with the Silhouettes?

Standing in line for lunch, I felt a light tap on the shoulder. I turned around. It was Heather Grant, another girl from Jennifer's clique.

"Jennifer told me to tell you since you're in The Fad you can sit with us."

I'd just been invited to eat lunch at Jennifer's table! Happy fireworks flared and sparkled in my head. I hoped they didn't show in my eyes. I wanted to look casual, like this happened every day. "Sure," I said.

On my way to the popular table, I paused at the usual

place where Claire and Joy and I ate lunch with a couple other girls from the outer fringe. Claire and Joy brought their lunches from home, so they were already sitting down.

"Uh, guys? I'm kind of having lunch at Jennifer's table today," I told them.

Joy glared up at me.

My shoulders slumped. "It isn't like that," I said quickly. "I'm just...I'm doing research for Evington's short story."

Claire didn't even look at me. She just opened her lunch bag and rooted through it.

"Come on, Claire," I pleaded. "I'll come over to your place tonight and we can do our homework together. Okay?"

"Whatever," she said in a bored voice.

"Go on," Joy said, still frowning at me. "Go flutter off with the other butterflies. We'll just stay here with the other dung beetles."

"Hey!" Claire said sharply. "Speak for yourself."

I bowed my head and shuffled away. Maybe I could make things up with Claire and Joy in our next class.

At Jennifer's table Hilary and Rachel sat near the head with Jennifer. Next came Stacy and Mica, Janine and Snooty Ella, and a few girls I didn't know. I eased into a seat toward the end, next to the girl who'd invited me to the table.

I got some halfhearted hi's from Jennifer's end of the table, but a couple of genuine-sounding greetings from the girls closer to me. They were obviously lower in the clique pecking order.

"So, what do your parents do?" one girl asked me. "My dad's an attorney."

I liked Eddie again now that he didn't seem to be drinking lately, so I borrowed him for a dad. Being a music professor might not impress anyone, though. I told the girl that my dad used to be on TV.

That got everybody's attention. Even Hilary's and Rachel's.

"Really?" girls squealed from all ends of the table. "What show?"

Eek! I hadn't thought far enough ahead. There was no way I could tell them it was a clown show for kids.

"It was a long time ago," I mumbled. "You probably wouldn't remember." My mind reeled, searching for a good lie to explain what he'd been doing since he left television. "Uh, he's in banking now," I added. At least he went to the bank to cash his paycheck from the college.

The girls nodded, satisfied for now, and went back to their favorite topic of conversation: clothes and celebrities. I was glad when lunch ended and I could be with Claire and Joy again.

On my way to geography Joy caught up to me. She asked in a friendly voice, "So, was it a good lunch?"

If she'd sounded mean I would've lied. But since she was acting like a best friend again, I confessed that it was pretty boring.

Joy put her arm around my shoulders. "I knew there was still hope for you."

I wasn't sure I liked the sound of that. It made me feel like I was one of Joy's psychology projects.

By eighth period I had forgotten all about being psychologized and writing short stories. It was time for the pep rally!

When the bell rang, the whole school filed into the gym. We were assigned different bleacher sections by grade, but we could sit with anybody in our section. Before I could figure out a way to tell Joy and Claire that I'd be sitting with the

Silhouette group, Joy nodded sympathetically. Even Claire smiled.

"You go ahead," Joy said. She sounded like a therapist again, being nice to a mental patient.

I frowned at her. "What are you up to?"

"Me?" Joy said in an innocent voice. "Nothing. Claire and I discussed it over lunch and we've decided to patiently wait for you to come to your senses." Joy peered at her watch. "We give you about an hour."

Annoyed, I walked away from my friends and crammed into the row filled with populars wearing Silhouette Racing Shoes. There were twenty-six of us. I counted.

The noise level in the gym began to get louder and louder. Soon the air was filled with confetti and happy voices. The marching band strutted down the middle of the basketball court, playing the school fight song. We leaped to our feet and cheered. Bass drum and trumpet sounds bounced off the brick walls and my heart thumped in time with the rhythm. Then the Silhouette row all put our arms around each other's shoulders. We swayed and cheered.

Domino, three rows down from me, looked back at me and smiled. Then Laraby Green, the kid sitting next to him, pulled something out of a big cardboard box. It was a silly blue and gold beanie with a propeller on the top. He handed beanies to everybody in his row. For half a second I thought Laraby was going to embarrass all his friends, including Domino. But suddenly there was a rush for the beanies. It turned out all the eighth graders wanted one. Even the popular kids.

Laraby gave out beanies until the box was empty. We flicked each other's propellers and laughed and cheered. We even cheered the principal, Mr. Beckett, when he stepped up to the microphone and introduced the football coach. Next, the coach called out the Blue Tigers' names, one by one. Each boy, in his blue and gold helmet and uniform, bounded across the basketball court. We screamed even louder.

Then the cheerleaders, all wearing Silhouettes, invited everybody wearing blue and gold laces to come down to the floor to cheer with them.

All twenty-six of us scampered over the bleachers and onto the court. The cheerleaders handed us extra pom-poms. But we populars weren't the only ones screaming our throats raw. The whole place vibrated with school spirit. Soon the cheerleaders motioned for the rest of the eighth grade class to come join us.

Chess club kids danced alongside beauty queens. Jocks laughed along with band members. For a while it didn't matter if you'd never been a class officer or a member of the pep club. It didn't matter if you had purple hair or a buzz cut. For that one hour everybody was popular. But of course it had to end. After the pep rally was over, the eager glow I'd felt faded as my throat grew sore from cheering. School spirit is great and all, but I couldn't help feeling a twinge of disappointment. I had felt special, wearing those Silhouettes. But I didn't feel special anymore.

Chapter Thirteen

I know you're not supposed to wait till the last minute to do homework, but on Sunday night I still hadn't come up with a short story idea for Mr. Evington's class. I had just opened to a blank page in my notebook when the phone rang. Mom yelled from the kitchen that the call was for me. I took it in Eddie's study.

A strange voice hissed through the receiver, "Strawberries. Tuesday."

I frowned at the wall. "What does that mean?" I said into the violin phone.

"Laces," the girl's voice whispered. "Strawberry. Just a few left. Ally's Attic. We're wearing them Tuesday."

The phone clicked dead in my ear. I stared at the phone long after I hung up. I rubbed my jaw a few times. Jennifer had promised to tell me if the clique changed the list. But *strawberries?* That sounded like kiddie laces.

Well, if that's where The Fad was headed, how could I argue?

I checked the clock. All the stores would be closed by now. If I wanted to buy a pair before Ally ran out, I'd have to go to Ally's Attic in the morning. I might have to miss a day of school to do it, but sometimes things couldn't be helped. On the plus side, if I skipped school tomorrow I wouldn't have to finish Mr. Evington's short story tonight.

I grinned, pleased with my own cleverness. I even had somebody who could write an absence excuse for me. Eddie.

The next morning I said brightly to Mom and Eddie, "It's such a nice day. I think I'll ride my bike to school."

"Watch the traffic," Mom said.

"Yup," I said, and skipped out.

I rolled my bike out of the garage. Domino was leaning against his mom's car, munching on a breakfast bar. He stood up and stuffed the bar in his jacket pocket.

"Ace!" he called. "You're riding to school today?"

"That's right," I said in a loud voice, in case anybody was listening from inside my house.

"Wait up, I'll ride with you."

Oh no. I shoved down my kickstand and darted after him. In Dom's garage I whispered, "You can't ride with me. I'm— I'm not exactly going to school."

Domino's eyes widened. "Really?" he said. He cracked up laughing. "Cool! I need a day off, too," he said. Dom swung his leg over his bike. "Where we goin'?"

"It probably should be just me," I said. "I wouldn't want to get you in trouble."

"But I want to come," he insisted.

I recognized that eager glow in his eyes. Last time he had it was when we were eight. He thought we could fly if we rolled down his sliding board wearing skates and a cape. Almost everything Domino did when he was eight involved either paramedics or angry moms.

"You'll get detention," I said.

"So? Where to?" he asked. Obviously he wasn't willing to take no for an answer.

"Ally's Attic."

"Ally's Attic?" Dom scrunched up his face. "Doesn't that store sell junk?"

I shrugged. "Well, it's kind of upscale junk. Probably too fancy for guys. You'd better just take the bus to school."

I dashed back to my bike and took off.

Two seconds later Domino coasted next to me. "I like fancy junk."

I ignored him. At the first red light, instead of turning right toward Wollerton, I pedaled left, toward Ram's Head College. Domino followed.

Ally's Attic was on Main Street. Since the shop was only a block from the college, Eddie drove by it every day. Now I was glad Dom had come along. It gave me an extra pair of eyes. I told Domino to be on the lookout for Eddie's car. It would be pretty bad if Eddie caught us. To be safe, we turned off Main and coasted along a parallel road.

Two blocks later we leaned our bikes against the back wall of Ally's Attic.

Dom grinned, showing off his chipped tooth. "This is like some kind of spy deal."

He peeked around the side of the stone building, scouting for Eddie's blue Escort. "All clear," he whispered.

We sneaked to the front. Ally's glass door was locked. The sign tacked to it said the shop didn't open until ten o'clock.

Oops. Domino and I looked at each other.

"Now what?" we said at the same time.

Since I was related—well almost—to a professor, I knew

the perfect place to hide at the college till Ally's store opened: The Ram 'n Eggs. That was a snack bar on the second floor of the dining hall. Most of the students just came in for take-out stuff. They had classes to attend. Unlike me and Domino.

It was a cozy little place, with dark paneled walls and maroon cushioned seats. When we strolled in, the overhead light was off. It took a few seconds for our eyes to adjust, even though sun splashed through a dozen big windows on the east wall.

The snack bar was practically empty. Only one of the five little tables in the center of the room was occupied. Two older ladies were drinking coffee and studying.

We ordered hot drinks from a skinny guy with acne and slid into a booth by a window. That way we could watch for suspicious activity outside. Like Eddie. But for now it looked safe. Nobody seemed to notice that two middle school kids had invaded their space.

I felt chilly in the snack bar. But maybe that was nerves. I had never skipped school like this before. Sure, I'd played the I-have-a-bellyache game a few times, but that was when Mom used to spend more time at home. I shivered a little and warmed my hands over the steam from my hot chocolate. I took a long swallow and almost relaxed.

Domino casually dumped five packets of sugar into his coffee. He acted like this was the most natural way to spend a day out of school.

"So," Domino said in a calm voice. "What do we need at Ally's?"

I almost choked on my drink. If he knew why we were on this mission he'd make that face of his at me. He was famous around school for his curled lip and wrinkled brow. For half a second I considered making up a story, but no lie came to mind. Dom would've seen through it anyway.

"Uh, strawberry laces," I murmured into my mug. I cringed, waiting for his are-you-out-of-your-mind? expression.

Domino jiggled his little finger in his right ear, as if a better answer might bounce against his eardrum if he cleaned it out.

"Look," I said, plunging into the truth. "One of the populars has been giving me secret information about shoelace combinations. Tuesday is strawberry day. Okay?"

Domino clapped his palm over his forehead. "We're skipping school for a dumb *fad?*" He stared at the ceiling and moaned, "We're gonna get busted over strawberry shoelaces."

I peered into my mug. Put that way, it did sound kind of stupid. "Well, when I came up with this idea I meant to go alone. Eddie does favors for me sometimes and I was thinking maybe he'd write me an excuse."

"Man," Domino said, "why didn't you tell me that before we left? Now if I get detention you won't be there to pass notes to."

I bowed my head even lower. "Sorry, Dom," I murmured. Then I popped my head up again with a sudden thought. "If you leave right now and hit all the lights right, you might make it back to school before third period. I'll be okay on my own."

Dom's eyes widened. "Are you kidding? We're having an adventure here. A lame adventure, but still... I mean, we won't be buying laces all day, right? We can finally hang for a while together without, you know, people sneaking up on us."

"True," I said, smiling. My insides swirled. I thought about the kiss. "We can go back to my house later," I offered. "Nobody will be there. Well, as long as Mom or Eddie doesn't come home for lunch, anyway."

"My place is definitely out," Dom said. "My mom caught that same bug your mom had last week, so she's there in bed. Hey! I know. We could go to my old tree house."

We both laughed. Back when we were little kids, Dom and I used to sit up there drinking lemonade and telling ghost stories. Now we could sit up there and…well, we'd see what happened once we got up there.

"First, we have to complete our shoelace mission," I said. I wasn't ready to think too hard about what we might do in the tree house. I didn't want to jinx any kissing.

"So what do strawberry laces look like, anyway?" asked Dom.

I shrugged. "I have no idea, but there aren't too many of them. That's why I got the secret call."

Dom finished his sugar-coffee in one swallow. "Ace, what if your spy is a double agent?"

I squinted at him. "Huh?"

"Maybe this spy is feeding you fake information to embarrass you again."

The possibility sent a jolt right through me. Dom was right. What if the strawberry info didn't really come from Jennifer? I hadn't actually recognized the whispered voice. And on top of that, why would she have to whisper over the phone anyway? Why couldn't she come straight out and say, "Hey, Asa, it's Jennifer. I have a tip for you in the shoestring department."

I sat there with my mouth open for a full minute.

"See? Makes sense, huh?" Dom said, all proud of himself.

I reached across the table and socked Dom in the shoulder, but not in a good way. "Thanks for ruining everything. Now I don't know if I should buy the stupid things or not."

Domino grinned. "Then let's just go back to the tree house."

"Wait," I said, stalling a little. The tree house thing was starting to make me nervous. Maybe we weren't ready for so much kissing yet. We'd be alone for hours. "Uh, it'll be okay," I said. "I'll get the laces but I'll keep them in my pack tomorrow. If nobody else is wearing strawberries, I won't be embarrassed. And if they are, I can switch laces real fast and still be in The Fad." I smiled back, feeling like a genius.

Dom shook his head. "Still don't know why you want all this stuff anyway."

"It's just something I need to try," I said in a small voice.

"Whatever." Domino shrugged.

At ten o'clock sharp we headed back to Ally's Attic. We were the first ones through the door after Ally switched the sign on the door from "Sorry, we're closed" to "Come in! We're open."

Ally practically greeted us at the door. The lines around her eyes crinkled in a happy way when we stepped inside.

"Good morning!" she said. "Do you kids need help finding anything today?"

My eyes zoomed in on Ally's jar of red licorice whips beside the register. Eddie's favorite candy. A stab of guilt poked me in the ribs.

"We're fine, thanks," I said. "Looking for shoelaces, but we know where they are."

I tugged Domino down the wreath aisle. "We have to find these things fast," I whispered.

"If you don't see what you want, just give a shout," Ally said from the front.

"Thanks," I called back.

I hurried past the stuffed teddy bears to the shoelace display. There were only a few pairs of laces decorated with strawberries. My spy was right about that part at least.

Domino pulled a shoelace packet from the hook and frowned at the printing. "This is crazy. They're *scented!*"

I huddled closer for a better look. He cracked open the seal. We both sniffed. Then we choked. The laces smelled like industrial strength strawberry bubble gum.

"Why would anybody want their shoelaces to smell like that?" I wondered out loud. Of course then I remembered Jennifer's handwriting. Maybe people who dotted their *i*'s with hearts liked this kind of thing.

Then I spotted the price. "Eight ninety-nine! They cost more than regular laces."

"Guess they charge extra for the smell," said Dom. "Are you sure you want to do this, Ace? This is totally beneath you."

"I know it is," I mumbled. I rooted through my pack for my wallet. "The part that bugs me," I said, still rummaging, "is the tax."

"Yeah? Well the part that bugs me—" Dom began.

That's all I heard. Just then a pointy finger thumped my right shoulder. I glanced behind me. Eddie stood there, smiling. He held a half-eaten licorice whip in his other hand. I almost dropped my backpack. *Busted!*

"Let me guess," Eddie said pleasantly. "Field trip?"

Right away my head told me, *Uh oh*. Then my legs said, *Run!*

I threw down the laces, clutched my pack, and bolted for the door.

"Didn't we have what you wanted?" Ally called out.

Domino raced after me. Neither of us looked back. We hopped on our bikes and started pedaling very, very fast. We zoomed all the way back to our neighborhood. Neither of us spoke.

Eddie didn't follow us. We never saw any blue Escorts on the road, anyway.

At the far end of Domino's yard, we hid our bikes in the hedge. Then we climbed into Domino's drafty little tree house. We sat on the damp wood with wind whistling through the uncovered window.

Now that we were safe, Dom cracked up laughing.

"Ha!" Dom said. "I think we broke the sound barrier."

I wanted to laugh, too. Except for one thing. That was *my* almost relative who'd caught us in Ally's Attic. What if Eddie decided to cancel his class so he could look for us? Would he yell at me like a real dad if he found us? Would he think to look up here? Did he even know Dom and I used to play in this tree house?

"Ace, lighten up," Dom said. "We ditched him."

"That's just it," I said. "When I go back home he could ground me for life. He could..." I gulped. "He could tell my mom."

Dom's face turned serious. "Oh, man. I forgot about that. Hey wait," he said, his face brightening. "I've got walkie-talkies. If Eddie grounds you and sends you to your room for life, we can call each other."

That made me feel a little better.

"But what about you, Dom?" I asked, suddenly remembering I wasn't the only one with parents who might get angry. "Will you be grounded?"

"Yeah, but it doesn't matter. I got this." Dom pulled a Game Boy Advanced out of his pack and powered it up. "When they ground me they always say, no music, no TV, but they forget all about this baby. Wanna play football? You can pick any NFL team you want."

I shrugged and scooted closer so I could see the tiny screen better. I thought we'd climbed to this private place in the tree to kiss. I was kind of disappointed but also sort of relieved. Dom picked the Philadelphia Eagles. I chose the Miami Dolphins. They were Mom's and my favorite team.

I'd started watching football when I was in fourth grade. At first I just did it because Mom made hot chocolate and popcorn for everybody. We'd all get comfy in the family room, Mom and Eddie snuggling close on the couch, and me curled up in an old beanbag chair. Sunday afternoons we'd spend hours and hours, watching football on TV. Pretty soon I started enjoying the games.

Dom and I sat on the hard floor, shoulder to shoulder, and played football till our stomachs started to growl. We pulled our bag lunches out of our packs, chomped on sandwiches, and kept playing. We played three Super Bowls. I won two. Then the wind turned chilly and the sun moved past the three o'clock position. We'd have to climb down soon and head home.

I nudged Dom. "If your parents ask what you did today, what will you tell them?"

He snorted. "I sure won't tell them my Eagles lost to your fish-heads!"

Then finally, after all that time alone in the tree house, we stared into each other's eyes. I felt a fluttery rush inside.

More wind whooshed through our tree. The limbs creaked. A chilly blast of air pushed Dom closer. He bent his head toward mine in slow motion. My brain kept screaming, *Kiss me, kiss me. Just do it already!*

His nose bumped into mine. I tried to get my nose out of the way but turned my head too far. Dom's cold lips brushed across my jaw. All of a sudden his watch alarm started tweedling. We both jumped apart.

"We gotta go," Domino said breathlessly. He shut up his watch with a push of a button. "I set that for exactly one minute before we usually get home from school. If we walk through our doors exactly on time people might not get suspicious." Dom elbowed me. "Hey Ace, we might actually get away with this!"

"Uh huh," I said, still shaken by our messed-up kiss. How come the first one felt so good and natural? This one was just plain...awkward.

"Come on, Ace," Dom said.

I snapped out of my daze. He was already on the first rung hammered into the tree trunk. I grabbed my pack and climbed down after him.

Dom waited for me at the bottom of the tree. "See ya," he said. He leaned toward me for a final kiss. It was better. At least this time our lips actually touched.

At exactly three-fifteen Dom and I rolled our bikes into our joint driveway. My heart lurched as I spotted Mom's car parked outside the garage. That wasn't right. Back in the old days her boss used to let her go home early. But lately, now that she was working extra overtime, she rarely came home before five-thirty.

I leaned my bike against the garage wall and sucked in a breath of air to calm my jangling nerves. *Act natural,* I told myself. I tried to pretend it was like the old days when Mom used to be home to greet me. I dropped my backpack on the dining table.

Mom stood behind the snack bar, drinking tomato juice.

"What a day," I said. That's what I always used to say when Mom was home.

She broke tradition by scowling at me with her green cat eyes. She set down her glass. "Why don't you tell me about your day?"

I ordered my shoulders to shrug in a nonchalant way. "Same old stuff. Boring lectures, lots of homework. Better get started." I lifted my pack.

"Where have you been?" Mom demanded angrily.

I gulped. I couldn't believe it. Eddie had told on me!

"What did he say?" I asked, fighting panic.

"What did who say? I spoke to Carol. She called my office this morning," Mom said in an icy voice. "She wanted to verify your absence from school."

I felt my stomach drop. Eddie hadn't ratted me out after all, but I was still in serious trouble here. How could I have forgotten that Mom knew the school secretary? It had started a couple years ago when I kept getting tonsillitis. Mom had to call in to the office a lot. Soon she and Carol were buddies. I'd never guessed the secretary would call my mom for one tiny absence.

"What did you, uh, tell Carol?" I asked.

"The truth," Mom said, still frowning. "When you left here this morning you were in perfect health. Carol and I had a nice chat. I understand that Domino also took the day off. Were you two together?"

I slumped into a dining chair. "Kinda."

"Were you drinking?" she demanded.

My head shot up. *"What?"*

Mom actually leaned over and checked my breath! It wasn't even fair. Mom never did that to Eddie and sometimes he really did have stuff on his breath. All Mom smelled on me was stale bubble gum.

"Well," she said, straightening up. "Then what exactly were you doing?"

A blaze of heat shot off in my face. Even though we'd only shared one and a half kisses, I still felt guilty. If Mom was suspicious about us drinking, what horrible things would she suspect about me and Dom being alone in a tree house all day?

"We just rode around on our bikes," I blurted. "Honest." That was partly the truth.

"We're not discussing this anymore right now," Mom said. She jammed her arms into her jacket. "I just wanted to make sure you were okay."

She snatched up her purse and car keys.

"I'm going back to the office now," she said. "You can explain yourself to your father. I already called and told him all about it."

My knees turned so weak they almost gave out. My *father* knew? He hadn't even sent as much as a postcard since he'd left. How could I explain anything to him? I didn't even know him anymore. Or worse, what if Mom made me go live with him—a total stranger? And all because of a stupid pair of strawberry shoelaces I didn't even buy.

At the door Mom said, "Don't you dare leave this house, Asa Marie. Your father will be home at four."

Alarm bells clanged in my head. Mom was going to leave me alone in the house with a person I hadn't seen in nine years? How did she even expect me to recognize him?

"My father's coming here?" I said. "My *father?* But—"

"Your stepfather, Asa," Mom said in disgust. The door slammed behind her.

I leaped up and yanked open the door. "Wait!" I cried out.

Mom stopped and glared over her shoulder at me.

"What did he say when you told him I cut school?"

Her frown deepened. "He said he'd handle it himself. Now go to your room and wait. You're grounded," she said, and stormed to her car.

He'd handle it. What did that mean? I puffed nervously and paced in the kitchen.

Mom had called Eddie my father. She'd never done that before. Had Eddie told her that he was going to be my father from now on or did Mom just make that up? What did the new title mean? Was he allowed to actually yell at me now? Except he hadn't told Mom he'd seen me at Ally's today. Did that mean we had one more secret to share?

Would we have a big laugh when he got home? Or was I in wait-till-your-father-gets-home trouble like on the TV sitcoms?

The wall clock above the refrigerator said I had exactly forty-two minutes before my "father" came home.

Chapter Fourteen

Even though Mom had sent me to my room, I didn't go. How could I just sit around in there, waiting to find out what kind of mood Eddie would be in when he came home? What if he screamed at me? I knew he had it in him. It was pretty scary when Eddie yelled at his students during the college jazz band rehearsal.

Pacing didn't relax my jumpy nerves. Neither did slow, deep breaths. A long hot soak in the tub might've calmed me down. But I didn't have time. Eddie was scheduled to blast through the door any minute.

I went down to the basement. If he was angry, this would be a better place to wait for him. Music always made him really mellow. I slid one of Eddie's jazz CDs into the stereo. Perfect saxophone music blasted from the speakers. After listening for a few minutes, I started to calm down. I lifted his sax from its stand in the corner. The mouthpiece looked like a goose's bill. That seemed right. I'd heard the band kids at school make honking noises with their saxes.

I blew into the mouthpiece. Nothing came out. I tried two more times. Still nothing, so I decided to fake it. I put the reed back in my mouth and pretended to play along with the CD.

During a screaming solo I clenched my eyes shut. I swung the sax in time to the music and pushed on the keys. This was definitely better than deep breaths.

Near the end of the solo I got a prickly feeling I wasn't alone. I opened my eyes. Eddie stood at the bottom of the staircase. He was leaning against the banister with his arms folded.

I shot across the room to the stereo and turned off the music.

"I was…uh, playing the blues," I said sheepishly.

Eddie didn't yell. He just stared at me.

I'm good at reading faces. Whenever Claire and I did homework together I always knew when she wanted to be serious or when she wanted to joke. One look in Mom's eyes and I could tell if she'd had a good drum practice. I used to think I could tell when Eddie was angry. But this time his expression was as clear as a tinted window.

He motioned for me to go upstairs. It made me think of Mr. Music, the mute musician.

I put the sax carefully back on its stand. At the top of the staircase Eddie nodded toward the family room. Still not a word. I scuffed across the carpet and plunked onto the couch. Eddie leaned against the door frame, staring down at his feet.

Even though he'd never yelled at home before, I had a feeling this time he was going to make an exception. When this yell came it would be loud. He was probably working himself up to it. He'd start with a big lecture about how important it was to have an education. He'd want to know how I planned to get into college if I didn't go to class. Then he'd probably add some crack about flipping burgers. If that was what I wanted, he'd say, then I should keep missing class.

I waited for the lecture to start. Eddie just kept examining his shoes.

Finally he looked up. "This isn't the first time you've pretended you didn't know me, Asa."

That wasn't how the lecture was supposed to start. He was supposed to ask me what I thought I was doing at Ally's Attic. He was supposed to yell at me for hanging out with the wrong crowd (even though I wasn't). He was supposed to be a regular bossy dad.

I could read Eddie's face now. The corners of his mouth drooped. His eyes looked sad enough to cry. I didn't want to say the wrong thing and hurt his feelings even more. If that happened, I'd have to call Mom. She was already angry. She'd be furious if I made her husband cry.

I stared into my lap, afraid to talk.

The clock over the mantle ticked. For ages, that was the only sound.

"Ponies," Eddie said finally.

I looked up. "Huh?"

"A few years ago you were crazy about ponies, remember?"

I nodded, but stayed alert. The lecture had to be coming now.

"Yeah," he said in a faraway voice. "I remember thinking if I gave you a pony for your birthday you'd love me for life."

My eyes bugged out. Eddie actually *thought* about me?

"But your mom wouldn't let me." Eddie smiled sadly. "I drove off on the sly and found a pony farm owned by some old guy and his wife. What was his name?"

"Henson," I said immediately. I remembered his crinkly smile and his fields of ponies. Even though I didn't know where this conversation was headed, I smiled a little. "You said you'd give me all the ponies on his farm."

Eddie laughed with me. "Always think big, Ace. But I couldn't even give you one. Not just your mom. Zoning laws. I asked old Henson if I could 'borrow' his ponies for your birthday. He agreed to play along. I drove you out there and told you they were yours."

Old Mr. and Mrs. Henson and their ponies lived in the middle of farm country. It took a really long time for Eddie to drive me there. The Henson place was at the top of a steep hill where the road turned into a dead end. Ponies wandered around everywhere, grazing in the shady backyard or in the open fields.

Each pony had a name. I think I patted every one of them that day. I helped Mr. Henson feed and water them. He let me groom them with a currycomb and brush. Some snuffled sugar cubes out of my palm. Eddie even lifted me onto a red pony's bare back. He stayed right there at my side with his arm around my waist so I wouldn't fall off. We didn't say much, just breathed in the summer air.

"That was the best day I ever had," I said truthfully.

"Me too," Eddie said, smiling. "For a few hours I got a real taste of being a dad. Found out how it felt to have a daughter."

I looked away. Something in the air told me the bad part was coming.

"At the end of the day you had a big grin on your face," said Eddie. "Your cheeks were bright pink from the sun. Clothes all dusty and smelling like ponies."

I didn't remember that part.

"But your smile didn't last," he went on. "Once you figured out those ponies weren't really yours."

I did remember that. The next day I put on my cowgirl hat and skipped down to the basement. Eddie was playing his acoustic guitar. I bounced in front of him, eager to drive out to Mr. Henson's to play with the ponies again. When he started making lame excuses, I realized that it had all been an act. I was crushed. Looking back, I'm not sure if I was more upset about the ponies or about Eddie lying to me.

"Why didn't you just tell me the truth?" I asked.

"I tried. You didn't seem to want to listen to anything I said after that. You avoided me for weeks."

"I was only nine," I said in a small voice.

"Still hurt," he said with a shrug. He looked out the sliding glass door. Even though it was late September, the leaves were still green outside. You could tell by the way they wiggled in the breeze that they were ready to turn orange.

"I never tried to win you over again," Eddie said.

He looked from the sliding glass doors to his feet again. "Your mother wanted me to have a talk with you. I'm supposed to be the parent today," he said. His head snapped up. "But that's not what I am, is it? You don't run away like that from a parent."

He turned on his heel and left the family room. A minute later the jazz saxophone music started in the basement. It wasn't from a CD. It didn't sound angry or mellow. It sounded disappointed.

My shoulders slumped. That wasn't how our talk was supposed to go. Eddie was supposed to yell dad things at me. He was supposed to tell me I'd better straighten myself out. Maybe even call me young lady. Then he'd send me to my room with strict orders that I couldn't use the phone or instant messaging on the computer. I'd hate him till dinner when he'd come tell me, "Sorry I had to be strict, Ace, but I love you and want you to get a good education." Then he'd kiss me on the forehead, give me a little hug, and we'd be friends again. That was how it was supposed to work, anyway.

A tear wobbled near the corner of my eye. I sniffed and headed to the kitchen, pretending Eddie's sad music didn't hurt.

I opened and closed cabinets but didn't really notice anything inside. Technically, it was Eddie's turn to make dinner. I pulled out the cookbook and flipped through the pages. I settled on making quiche and tossed salad. I even made the piecrust from scratch.

At dinner Eddie only managed a half smile across the table for Mom. I didn't even get a side-glance. Nobody spoke till Mom asked, "So, did you two talk?"

Eddie shrugged and jabbed at his salad.

"I'm grounded for a month," I announced.

Mom turned toward me. She looked impressed. "You are?"

Eddie looked up. His eyes widened in surprise.

"I'm under strict orders to come straight home after school," I said, carefully following Joy's lying lessons in my mind. "I'm supposed to help with any house cleaning. Then I have to stay in my room till my homework's done…and checked for accuracy. Oh, and no TV or phone privileges."

"Whoa, Eddie!" Mom said, laughing. "When you go parental you don't mess around, do you?"

"Well, you know," he said modestly.

"If I keep out of trouble, I can get off on good behavior in two weeks," I said.

"Incentive," Eddie said, playing along, "to follow the straight and narrow."

Mom nodded, still smiling. "I like it."

Eddie's cheeks turned bright pink. This time when he looked at his plate his dimples showed.

Chapter Fourteen

After dinner I filled the dishwasher and sent myself to my room. I still had to write my short story for Mr. Evington. Since Eddie had brought it up, I decided to write about the day he took me to the pony farm. I made the beginning seem like the grown-up and the little kid in the car were strangers. Then at the pony farm they gradually changed from strangers to a little family.

Okay, so I gave them a sugary, happily-ever-after ending. Blame that on the fact that I needed my creativity for something else. I wanted to think up a good written excuse to take to school. It had to be clever since Mom and Carol, the attendance secretary, had already talked to each other.

My head still ached from the whole shoelace episode. That gave me an idea. Sometimes headaches meant eyestrain. An eye doctor appointment was a perfect reason to miss class. I jotted it down in a note. Now all I needed was a parent's signature.

I heard Mom start her car to drive to her Al-Anon meeting. I waited till the car sounds faded away. Then I poked my head through Eddie's open study door. He was typing his evening e-mail to Poppy. He paused to look across the room at me.

"What's that?" He nodded at the paper I nervously fingered. "An assignment I'm supposed to check?" He grinned. "Nice job at dinner, by the way."

I shook my head. I stepped deeper into the room. "This is—" I hated asking questions that would probably get a no for an answer. "It's sort of an excuse. To give to the attendance secretary."

His brow wrinkled into a baffled frown.

"You know. To explain why I was absent," I finished, all in one breath.

Eddie held out his hand. I laid the paper across his palm. He leaned back in his swivel chair. "'Dear Carol,'" he read out loud. "'Please excuse Asa Philips for being absent from school yesterday. After her mom went to work, Asa said she had a headache from eye strain—'" Eddie looked over the page at me. He went back to reading. "'—so I took her to my job with me. On a free period I drove her to the eye doctor for a checkup. Since her mom didn't know we were at the eye doctor's, she didn't know Asa was absent when you called. Very truly yours, Edward C. Clegg (stepfather).'"

Eddie sat up. He put the paper on his desk. "That's not how I remember it, Ace."

"Well...we couldn't say the real reason. Not to the attendance secretary."

He raised an eyebrow. "Then say the real reason to me. What were you doing at my end of town?"

"Looking for shoelaces."

Eddie looked like he had just bit into a bad oyster. "Shoelaces? Are you still doing that fad thing?"

I shifted my weight from one foot to the other. "Well..."

"This shoelace business has to stop, Asa." He sounded just like a stern dad now.

"It will," I said. "I'll never buy another pair."

"Wise decision," Eddie said with a nod. He turned back to his computer.

"Um, about that excuse," I said. "I still need one. So I won't get detention."

His chair squeaked as he swiveled toward me again.

"Do I really need detention?" I asked. "I mean, I already grounded myself for two weeks."

"A month."

"Two weeks if I'm good," I reminded him.

"One month if I go along with this scheme of yours," Eddie muttered. He skimmed the note a second time. "Needs some editing. And I guess I'll have to copy it over in my handwriting," he added, almost to himself.

Relief and hope lifted my shoulders. "You'll do it?"

"For a price, maybe," Eddie said.

My shoulders dropped again. "I only have six bucks."

"I'm not talking about money." He pulled a flask out from under some papers in his desk drawer and handed it to me. "Fill this from the bottle in your closet, okay? We'll trade tomorrow when Mom isn't looking. Your note for my flask. Deal?"

I froze. Not another deal. This one didn't even make sense. The last time I stuck my hand into the back of the closet Eddie's hidden bottle still had an unbroken seal. For the past few weeks Eddie had been his regular, sober self.

I took a deep breath. "I thought—I thought you didn't need...the little people anymore." I almost whispered the last part.

"Oh," Eddie said, fidgeting a little. "Yeah. Well. It's not exactly for me. I like to keep a flask at work. In case—" He paused. "In case the dean of music should come by my office. He likes a nip now and then."

I stared at the floor. "Uh huh," I mumbled.

"Look, Ace, gimme a break, okay?" Eddie pleaded. "It's not like I'm a wino in the gutter. I'm in complete control here. Look at this." He held out his right hand. "Like a rock."

I blinked at his steady hand.

"You know how crazy your mother gets about alcohol. There's no need to get her all upset for nothing. Anyway,"

Eddie said, lowering his hand, "like I said, most of it's for the dean. So, do we have a deal?"

Without that note I'd have a detention on my permanent record. Even if Domino would be there to keep me company, I still didn't want a bad record.

I nodded sadly.

Eddie drove me to school the next morning. He slid a folded piece of paper out of his jacket pocket and handed it over.

"Got something for me?" he asked.

I pulled his flask out of my pack.

"Thanks, love," he said with a smile. It was the first time he'd ever called me that. A twinge of guilt rumbled through me. Maybe I shouldn't have watered down the stuff in his flask. But I had to.

I knew a very big secret now. Eddie was out of control.

Chapter Fifteen

Eddie dropped me off at the front entrance of the school, way ahead of my bus. One of the populars named Amy strolled into the building two seconds ahead of me. My eyes quickly zoomed in on her feet. She was wearing suede boots.

If this was supposed to be Strawberry Day, where were Amy's Silhouette Racing Shoes? Domino was right! There was a double agent in Jennifer's group trying to give me fake information so I'd look stupid. My mind rang with a self-satisfied, *Ha!* Hooray for me for not buying those smelly laces in the first place. Since I had gym today, my feet were safely wrapped in a pair of normal, non-embarrassing tennis shoes.

Hilary and Rachel strolled by my locker a few minutes later. They were both wearing bright pink, all the way down to their shoes. So they weren't wearing strawberries either. I figured if they were the double agents they would check my feet to see if I'd fallen for the prank. Nope. They didn't even glance in my direction.

A second later Joy popped up behind me and clapped me on the back. "All right, Asa!" she said. "Way to go! I was afraid when you were absent yesterday that you were out buying strawberry laces."

I gasped as I spun around. "How did you know about that?"

Joy put her hand over her mouth and said in a muffled voice, "Strawberries. Tuesday. Just a few left." She pressed her lips together in a smug smile.

"That was *you?*" I squealed. "You're supposed to be my friend! Would you actually try to make a fool out of me?"

"It was a test," Joy said, "to see if you could still be swayed by peer pressure." She nodded toward my tennis shoes. "See? You passed!" She hugged me. "You're back to normal again."

Just then Claire rushed up to us. "It was cramps, right, Asa? Say it was cramps. You didn't cut school for laces, did you?"

I slumped against my locker. "So were you in on it, too?"

Claire shook her head. "I knew about it, but I told Joy *not* to call you," she said. She directed a heated stare at Joy.

"It's called intervention," Joy said in her psychologist's voice.

"No, it's called a dirty trick," I said. "Lucky for you I have an excuse right here," I added, patting my pack. "And I'm on my way to hand it in right now. See you in homeroom."

I was furious with Joy. And with Claire, too, for not warning me. But right now I had other worries. What if Eddie's written excuse wasn't good enough for the attendance secretary?

On my way to the office I checked Eddie's note to make sure he hadn't watered it down like I did his flask. Eddie had changed a few sentences, but the excuse was basically the same. I let out a relieved sigh.

"Ace, wait up!" Domino shouted from the other end of the crowded hall. He bobbed and weaved around bunches of kids to catch up.

I backed away from the office door, glad for the delay.

"Hey," said Dom, thumping my arm. "Did Eddie give you an excuse?"

I nodded. "I was just about to drop it off." I showed Dom
the note.

"Eye doctor," he said after he read it. "Sweet. Your secret's
safe with me, by the way." Dom handed back the note. "I
told my parents I cut school 'cause I hadn't finished a report
that was due yesterday. They grounded me for a week, plus
whatever punishment the vice principal gives me. A couple
days detention, probably."

"No fair!" I told him. "I'm giving up a month's worth of
TV and phone privileges for this."

"No problem," Dom said with a grin. "I have a solution."
He pulled a walkie-talkie out of his pack and passed it over.
"Turn it on tonight at eight-thirty."

At first the idea of using walkie-talkies for a conversation
with Dom seemed kind of silly. But in a way it was almost
like a date. That made it sort of romantic. I stuffed the
walkie-talkie in my own pack and promised I'd tune in at
eight-thirty sharp.

The warning bell rang. Dom waved and hurried toward
his homeroom. I gathered my courage and stepped into the
attendance secretary's office. I cringed on the inside as I
handed her my excuse. Mom didn't exactly know about this
note. If the secretary called her, Eddie and I would both have
a lot of explaining to do.

"Well, look at this," she said, peering through her half-
glasses at Eddie's note. "I'll bet your mother must feel terrible. She thought you were out gallivanting yesterday."

"Yeah, my stepdad and I straightened out that little mis-
understanding," I said, then held my breath. She pulled out
her roll book and marked my absence "Excused."

My legs felt weak from relief. I'd done it!

"Thanks," I said. As long as I never missed school again, maybe she and Mom'd have no reason to talk on the phone.

I glided back to homeroom and floated on clouds the rest of the day. I even forgave Joy and Claire for the mean strawberry prank. I didn't even mind the mini-lecture Mr. Evington gave me for handing in my short story in longhand instead of printing it out from a computer.

"The next draft must be typewritten," he told me.

After school, I was the only one who got off at my bus stop. Dom had told me between classes that he'd be stuck in detention for three days, not two. That left nothing for me to do at home but homework.

I scurried to Eddie's study before he came home and typed my short story into his computer. The last page had just rolled from the printer when the phone rang. It was Eddie, calling from the college. "I got stuff going on, Ace," he told me over the phone. "I should be home around ten. Okay?"

"Okay," I said.

Stuff was Eddie's code word for playing in Frizzy Guy's band. I guessed that's what it meant, anyway. On Tuesdays, when Mom drove straight from her office to paralegal class, Eddie usually called to tell me he had stuff going on.

Today was supposed to be my first day of being grounded. But if no parents would be home to see me...

"And don't forget, you're grounded," Eddie said, almost as if he'd read my mind. "You stay in the house, Asa." He sounded like a stern dad again.

"I'm not going anywhere," I promised. That was the honest truth. After we hung up I pounced on the phone to invite Claire and Joy over for homework and pizza.

For the first half hour we really did do homework. The

three of us sat at the dining table with our math books open, pencils scratching over notepaper. Except for a few pretzel munching sounds and gulps from our water bottles, we were quiet as a library. Mom would've been proud.

I flipped the page for the second half of my assignment. Word problems. I hated word problems. They turned simple math into a complicated mess. The first one was about a farmer with a hole in his bucket. I read it three times and still didn't get it. Why would a farmer add up trips to the well? He could plug the hole with chewing gum and make just one trip.

I studied my sixteen-ounce bottle of spring water. How fast would it empty if it had a hole in it? I scooted to the kitchen bulletin board for a pushpin and returned to my chair. I jammed the pin into the plastic, then pulled it out again.

Confession: I had hoped for water to shoot through the little hole and spray Joy. Instead, it dribbled down the side of the bottle and onto my lap.

I leaped from my seat.

Joy looked up. "Asa, what are you doing?"

"I'm a farmer with a hole in my bucket."

"Yeah? Well..." A naughty grin spread across Joy's face. "Hey look, I'm a fireman!"

She squeezed her own open bottle from the middle. I ducked. A stream of water spurted across the table, hitting Claire in the chest.

"Stewart!" Claire protested. "You'll get our books wet."

Joy practically fell off her chair laughing.

"I'm a little rain cloud," I said, and dumped the rest of my water on Joy's head.

That's when the water battle really got going. We squealed and doused each other till we ran out of spring water. Then we raced to the sink. At least we kept to the tile floors in the kitchen and dining areas. Joy filled a saucepan from the sink and chased us till Claire slid in a puddle and knocked down two dining chairs. Joy and I collapsed on top of her. We giggled till our stomachs ached.

Unfortunately, good times never last long. This time the phone interrupted the fun.

"Nobody say anything!" I said, untangling myself. "You're not supposed to be here, remember?" I sprang to the wall phone by the snack bar.

Joy and Claire clapped their hands over their mouths. I tossed a roll of paper towels at them.

"Hello?" I said into the phone. I hoped I sounded casual.

Claire silently righted the chairs. Joy tore sheets from the paper towel roll and tossed them at the water spots.

"Hi, sweetie," Mom's voice sang over the phone. "Put your dad on, please."

I gulped. Two major thoughts collided in my head. One: When did Mom promote Eddie to *Dad?* And Two: It didn't matter what she called him. He still wasn't here.

"Um, who?" I said, stalling for time. "Oh, you mean Eddie?"

"No, I meant Ben Franklin," she retorted. "Of course I meant Eddie."

I turned my eyes toward Joy, the lie expert. I mouthed the words, "Where's Eddie?" She mouthed something that looked like "Batman." I squinted at her. A second later I got it.

"Bathroom! Yeah. He took the crossword puzzle. I think he'll be a while."

Joy gave me a thumbs-up and went back to mopping the floor.

"Oh, okay, no problem," said Mom. "When he comes out, tell him we need a roll of stamps. I planned to stop at the post office during lunch today, but never got a chance."

"A whole roll?" I said. I felt like I was living inside a math word problem.

One roll equals a hundred stamps. One stamp costs thirty-seven cents. If Asa Philips has only six dollars, how many times is she allowed to kick her stepfather in the shins to make up the difference?

It was bad enough covering for Eddie so Mom wouldn't get mad that I was home alone. Now I had to spend my own money for stamps *he* would be buying if he had come home on time like he was supposed to.

"You sure we need a whole roll?" I asked. The money to pay for those stamps was just as invisible as the fake dad in the bathroom doing crosswords.

"Positive," said Mom. "We're completely out. And remind him the phone and electric bills need to go out today. He can mail them while he's at the post office. Okay?"

"Sure," I said in a dull voice. How was I going to pull this off? Eddie, and his wallet that could afford stamps, wouldn't be home till ten.

"Thanks, sweetie. Gotta run."

Mom hung up. For a few seconds I stood with the phone pressed to my ear.

"Is your mom coming home early?" asked Claire, starting to gather her books.

I put down the phone. "No."

"Is Eddie?" asked Joy.

The sound of his name jolted me back to life. I tore down the hall to his study. If Mom knew the bills were due, so did

Eddie. Maybe he'd already written the checks and they were just waiting to be shoved into their envelopes. I yanked open drawers and slammed them shut until I found the checkbook. I lifted the vinyl cover and skimmed the register. In the past week Eddie had paid the water and sewer bills and Mom's subscription to *Modern Drummer.* There were no entries for the phone or electric bills.

Joy and Claire appeared in the doorway.

"Asa, what happened?" asked Joy. "Is everything okay?"

I opened a bottom drawer. The envelopes for the phone and electric bills sat on top, waiting for their checks. I slumped into Eddie's swivel chair.

"We have a small problem."

Joy raised an eyebrow.

"First," I said, "I need to buy a hundred stamps at the post office."

"That's okay, we'll go with you," Joy said with a shrug.

Claire nodded.

"Second, all I have is six dollars."

Claire and Joy pooled their money. I scowled at the pile of cash now on Eddie's desk. If we bought stamps we couldn't afford pizza for dinner. Even when Eddie was missing, he ruined things.

"It's okay, Asa," said Claire. "Who needs pizza?"

I nodded, even though it wasn't okay. Why did Eddie cause so much trouble?

"Oh, and one more thing," I said. "Mom wants Eddie to pay some bills today."

Joy grinned and cracked her knuckles. "These hands can forge any signature. Just show me a sample of his handwriting."

"You can't do that!" Claire screeched. "It's illegal!"

"It's his check, paying his bill," said Joy. "Nobody'll look twice at the signature."

"No," I said.

"Finally," said Claire, throwing up her hands. "The voice of reason."

"I meant no to Joy," I said. "If anybody forges Eddie's signature, it has to be me."

"Asa, are you crazy?" said Claire.

Joy beamed at me. "Every kid should learn how to forge her dad's signature."

"It's for a good cause," I said. "Otherwise I wouldn't do it."

I checked my watch. The post office closed in half an hour. If I wanted to keep Mom happy—and me and Eddie out of major trouble—I had no choice. I pulled out a cancelled check and a sheet of paper. Eddie's loops and squiggles weren't hard to imitate. It took a dozen practice signatures to get it right. I held my breath as I filled out the register and the two checks.

Claire and Joy bent their heads over my finished work.

Joy patted my shoulder. "Good job."

Claire sighed. "Good luck."

We scampered to our bikes and raced to the post office, bursting through the swinging doors five minutes before closing. I bought the roll of stamps and tore it open. My shaky fingers slapped stamps on the electric and phone bill envelopes. I popped them through the mail slot. Mission accomplished!

Back home we rooted through the kitchen cupboards for dinner. We settled for popcorn and chocolate ice cream. It wasn't pizza, but it still tasted good.

Just after dark Joy and Claire put on their jackets. On their way out I promised I'd pay them back for the stamps. They waved and stepped into the chilly night.

Now that I was alone, dark guilty thoughts crashed down on me. I tried to keep my mind occupied by straightening up the kitchen, but before I knew it, I was crying into the dishtowel. Why couldn't I live in a normal family with a normal dad who paid bills and bought stamps?

By eight-thirty I was feeling even more miserable. I dropped onto the couch in the family room and flicked on Domino's walkie-talkie. It hissed for a second before Dom's voice came through the little speaker. "Asa Diamonds, Asa Hearts, are you there? Over." The sound was a little distorted, but I still heard Domino's cheerful tone.

His happy energy should have made me smile. Instead, it made my eyes tear up again. I sniffed and swallowed down the heavy blob in my throat. Why did I feel so sad all the time? And how could Dom, who was grounded like me and had just gotten out of detention, sound so happy?

I pushed the talk button and said, "Here I am. Over." I fought back a sob.

"Hey, I looked out the window earlier and saw you and Claire and Joy riding your bikes. You're parents aren't home, are they?" asked Dom. "Over."

I sighed. "Mom's at night school," I told him. "And Eddie's doing…stuff. Over."

"Man, you are so lucky, Ace. Oops! Gotta go. Somebody's coming. See ya tomorrow. Over and out."

"Yeah, over and out," I murmured.

Dom thought *I* was lucky. I snorted at that idea. If I was so lucky, how come Eddie owed me stamp money? If I was so lucky, how come Eddie and I were always lying for each other?

And the lies weren't over, either. I had one more thing to do.

I pulled myself off the couch and trudged to the dining room. Using my new forgery technique, I wrote a note for Mom that read, "Bills paid! Love, Ed." I even scribbled it on the back of an old envelope the way Eddie did when he wrote little love notes to Mom. I also propped it against the salt-shaker in the middle of the dining table, just like always.

That saved Eddie from trouble with Mom. But it didn't save him from trouble with me. To teach him a lesson, I opened Eddie's secret bottle and flushed the contents down the toilet. Then, since the booze looked like water anyway, I refilled the bottle from the kitchen tap.

Eddie's car pulled into the drive at exactly five minutes till ten. He was right on schedule. He's even timed it so his car would be done making its popping, cool-down sounds before Mom came home at eleven.

I forgot to shut the bathroom door while I brushed my teeth. I heard the back door open and I glared at the faucet, hating him. Eddie thought he was so clever, coming home ahead of Mom, pretending he'd never left. His car keys clinked onto the dining table. A few seconds later I heard the swish of corduroy pant legs coming down the hall. From the corner of my eye I saw him appear in the open doorway.

I whirled to face him. He held the forged note in his hands. "Put that back!" I squawked, toothpaste spattering from my mouth.

He frowned at it. "What does this mean?"

"It means what it says," I said, around the toothbrush in my mouth. "Put it back so Mom knows you paid the bills."

"I don't think I did," Eddie mumbled, backing out of the room.

I snorted and shook my head. The guy was impossible. I rinsed.

Just as I started to floss, Eddie came back. This time he held the checkbook. "It almost looks like my writing," he said, staring at the register, "but it isn't." Eddie looked up. "Mind telling me what's going on?"

I told him in twenty-five words or less. The first few words made his eyes pop wide open. Toward the end his body melted into relief. He stepped into the room and hugged me. "Asa, you're an angel!"

I frowned. I didn't feel like an angel. "You owe me for a roll of stamps."

"You bought stamps, too?" Eddie looked pleased.

"No, you did." I held out my palm. Eddie pulled his wallet from his hip pocket. He handed over two twenty-dollar bills. "Keep the change," he said.

"I'm not going to say thank you," I told him. "Because I'm not speaking to you anymore."

That should have hurt his feelings. He just grinned. "As long as you don't tell Mom about it, I don't mind." He kissed the top of my head and strutted out.

I'd always wanted a dad to kiss me good night, but not like that. I furiously finished flossing. Eddie needed a stronger lesson than water in his vodka bottle. He needed somebody bigger and meaner than me, someone with hair redder than mine to yell at him.

Somebody like my mom.

But lately Mom was too busy to see what was going on around here. If she knew, she'd yell. But I wasn't ready to tell her.

Not yet, anyway.

Chapter Sixteen

O n Tuesday morning, during week three of my being grounded, Mom poked her head into my room. I was just zipping up my jeans skirt when she asked me to ride my bike to school so I could meet her at her office afterwards.

"Why?" I asked.

"Oh, I just thought we could spend a little time together," Mom said, smiling. "You know, just us girls."

I got the feeling Mom was up to something. "Am I allowed to do that when I'm still grounded?" I asked. I didn't really care about grounding rules. I just didn't want to have to change my outfit. Bike riding days meant long pants and all my jeans were in the laundry.

Mom winked and flashed another quick smile. "We'll make an exception," she said and closed my door.

I grumbled to myself. Now I had to start all over again.

There's a science to picking out what to wear for school. Never wear a white shirt on pottery day. Don't wear too many layers when you have gym. Never wear the same colored socks two days in a row even if they're different pairs.

I always lay something out the night before so I don't have to think about it in the morning when I'm still half asleep. Last night I had set out my jeans skirt and multistriped sweater, but now they were no good. By the time I settled on an old pair of gray jeans and a pink turtleneck, I only had enough time to grab a raw Pop-Tart for breakfast.

I rolled my bike out of the garage, still chewing.

"Ace, where are you headed today?" Domino called from his side of the driveway.

"School. Where else?"

"No more laces?"

I frowned at him. "Just get your bike and come on."

A minute later we coasted, side by side, toward town. At the first red light Domino looked over. "So what are you doing tonight?"

I just gave him a squinty stare. He knew from our nightly walkie-talkie chats that I was still grounded from when we ditched school.

Domino grinned. "Oh yeah, you're still rotting in jail. Think you can sneak out tonight? I got this new video game I want to show you."

Mom had night school again. And after the stamp incident, Eddie seemed to have less "stuff" to do. But even though he came home early, he spent most of his time in the basement, playing electric guitar. I probably could do some sneaking if I wanted.

"What time?" I asked.

Domino's eyes lit up. "Cool! You'll come?"

"Maybe. I'll try, anyway."

"It'll be great, Ace," Dom said. "My parents are going out to dinner tonight."

My heart fluttered. "You mean we'll be...alone?"

Domino laughed at me. "What's the matter? Are you scared or something?"

"Course not," I said. My voice sounded normal but my insides fluttered. Even though we hadn't kissed since the day in the tree house, I knew we would again. And tonight the two of us would be all alone in a real house.

"Jason's going to be there," Dom said, as if he'd read my mind. "But he's in the middle of reading a trilogy. He probably won't leave his room all night."

I wanted to ask what Dom meant by that, but the light changed. Domino zoomed across the intersection without looking back. I caught up to him a block later but we didn't talk the rest of the way. It was mostly uphill.

At school we chained our bikes to the stand at the back of the building.

"Don't come over till seven-fifteen," Dom said. "They said they were leaving at seven."

So he definitely didn't want his parents to know about me coming over. Did that mean we'd be doing more than just playing video games in his basement? That question played in my mind all morning.

By English class I could barely concentrate. I think Mr. Evington was talking about our short story assignment. He mentioned something about never giving out letter grades on creative writing projects. Anybody who did the assignment would get a check mark instead. That should have been good news. Except my mind kept bouncing from *What if Dom tries to kiss me?* to *What if he doesn't?*

"Fiction is completely subjective," Mr. Evington droned on.

Maybe Dom really only wanted to play video games and turn the stereo as loud as it would go while his parents were out. But then again…what exactly would he try? Just kissing? Or maybe even an accidental elbow brush against my blouse?

"Asa Philips," Mr. Evington said in a lively voice.

My head shot up. I felt my cheeks burn. Was I supposed to answer a question?

Before I could blurt out "Keats" (always a safe answer in Evington's class—Keats is his favorite poet), the teacher smiled at me from the front of the room and said, "Well done."

My heart did the panic shuffle. Could Mr. Evington read minds? Did he know I was thinking about kissing and stuff?

"Huh?" I said weakly.

Joy batted me on the shoulder with a rolled-up piece of notebook paper. "Wake up," she whispered. "He gave your story two check pluses," she whispered.

I couldn't believe it. My pony farm story got two pluses?

"It was such a touching tribute to blended families," Mr. Evington said, still smiling. "You could actually feel the deep yearning these two characters felt about building a relationship with each other."

You could? Ha. Then my story really was two-plus fiction. In real life I didn't think Eddie yearned for anything but music. Or maybe that bottle in the back of my closet. That's how it seemed lately, anyway.

Next Mr. Evington complimented Jake Fallon on his story about a haunted house. Then the teacher moved on to noun clauses. I went back to thinking about Domino.

At lunch I said casually to Claire and Joy, "Do you guys have any dating advice?"

Claire's milk carton fell out of her hand. Luckily, only a few drops spilled. Joy stopped peeling her banana.

"You have a *date?*" they both asked at the same time.

"Maybe," I said.

Joy went back to peeling her banana. "Maybe doesn't count."

Claire mopped her spilled milk with a mitten somebody had left on the empty chair beside her.

"There's this guy," I said. "Let's call him Guy X." My borderline crush on Domino was still a secret, even from my best friends. "He invited me to his house to play video games. I like him and I think he likes me but—"

"Aren't you supposed to be grounded?" asked Claire.

"Is Guy X Nate Simmons?" asked Joy. "I think he was watching you in history."

"Never mind who it is and never mind about being grounded," I said impatiently. "I need to know if I was invited as a date or as a friend."

"If you're only playing video games," said Claire, "it's as a friend."

"His parents won't be home," I added.

"Then it's a date," Joy said. She popped a piece of banana into her mouth.

"But his older brother will be there."

"Friendly visit," said Claire.

"What if the older brother spends the whole time reading in his bedroom?" I asked.

"No," said Joy. "That would make it a date. I was right the first time."

I turned to Joy. She could sound like an expert on just about anything even when she didn't know a thing about the subject. "Do you think I should dress sexy or wear something comfortable?"

"Sexy, definitely," she answered, without hesitation.

"Then my next question is, *how* sexy?" I asked. "I don't

exactly own anything...well, strapless or backless or, you know, sheer."

"Yikes!" said Claire. "Don't wear anything sheer! You'll be asking for trouble."

"Maybe something slightly lacy—" Joy stopped talking and looked at the end of our table.

A sixth-grade boy was standing there, stiff as a butler from a Victorian novel. He held up a half-pint carton of orange drink. "Is someone here named Asa?" he asked.

I pointed at myself.

He bowed. "This is for you," he said and handed me the carton. Sixth-graders will do almost anything for a buck. They'll even pretend to be a waiter. "Compliments of the gentleman two tables over," he added.

I looked in the direction the kid pointed. Domino grinned and waved at me. My cover was blown. I smiled back and held up my orange drink.

Joy bent across the table. "Guy X is Dominic Weber?" she said in horror. "I thought you meant you had a date with a human."

Even Claire looked surprised. "Didn't you tell me he used to look up your skirt when you got on the school bus?"

"That was second grade!" I cried out. I knew this was how my friends would react. That was why I'd never told them in the first place. But now that it was in the open I had to defend him. "Dom's different now," I said. "More mature."

"Since when?" asked Joy. "He made armpit noises in music class last week."

"Since he kissed me," I said.

That shut them up.

"The gentleman also wondered," said the waiter, "if he

might have the pleasure of the company of two of your mom's peanut butter cookies."

I'd forgotten the kid was still there. In a romance novel, I thought, Dom would have requested the pleasure of *my* company. I swallowed the disappointment and rooted through my lunch bag. Mom didn't have time to cook anymore. I handed two store-bought cookies to the sixth-grader. "They're chocolate chip, but the gentleman likes those too."

The waiter kid bowed and strode to Domino's table.

I opened my orange drink. "What do you think that all meant?" I asked. "Girlfriend or friend?"

"It's called trading," said Joy. "Dress for comfort tonight. You're not getting any romance from that guy."

I looked two tables over at Domino. He was still grinning at me. I knew the answer now. Tonight was definitely going to be a date.

Chapter Seventeen

After school all the lights were green for me on the way to Mom's office. I biked there in record time. I couldn't imagine why Mom had asked me to come by today of all days. Could she have had some sixth sense that her grounded daughter was planning to sneak out tonight? No. I didn't think so. Whatever it was, I hoped she wouldn't expect me to stay too long. There were a thousand things I had to do to get ready for my date with Domino.

Mom saved two minutes by waiting for me in the lobby.

"Hi, kiddo," she greeted me as I burst in. She was wearing her reading glasses like a headband again. At least this time the frames pushed all her hair back in the same direction.

Mom said we could use the conference room on the first floor. "More private," she said over her shoulder as I followed her in.

I was glad we wouldn't be distracted by ringing phones. That meant no interruptions. If we talked fast enough I could be out of there in fifteen minutes.

Since it was sort of her break, Mom brought a cup of coffee for herself and a can of ginger ale for me. She set them both on paper napkins so we wouldn't make water rings on the shiny glass tabletop.

"So here we are," Mom said after we had settled into two

padded chairs at one end of the long, conference table. "How is everything, honey?"

I just said, "Fine." That's about all I could handle since most of my brain was thinking about Domino. Our date was only a few hours away. I had to shower, wash my hair, choose an outfit. I peeked under the cuff of my jeans to see if I needed to shave my legs on top of everything else. Definitely.

"Asa?"

I looked up from my ankle.

"Could you be a little more specific?"

I had to tell Mom something, so I mentioned the two pluses Mr. Evington had given me on my short story assignment in English.

"That's great, Asa!" Mom said. "When do I get to read it?"

I stopped smiling. The ending had the little kid in my story calling the guy "Daddy." Mom was already referring to Eddie as Dad behind his back. I didn't want her getting any ideas and doing that in front of him. I didn't think anybody was ready for that yet.

"It's kind of a dumb story, Mom. About, uh, ponies."

"Sweetie." Mom brushed her fingers gently through my hair. "Of course I want to read it. I'm busy, but I still care about you. That's why I asked you to come today. We need to spend more time together. Before we know it you'll be away at college."

I thought maybe she was rushing things a bit. I hadn't even started high school yet. I took a drink of my ginger ale. The bubbles tingled all the way down my throat. What did Mom really want?

"Want me to tell you a little about what I'm doing?" she asked in an eager voice.

I nodded. Her face was glowing with excitement.

"Well, I'm having such a blast at night school," Mom said, her eyes glistening, "that I was thinking, if we had the money, I might change over and go to law school! I'm writing briefs here at work and doing research. You have no idea how fascinating some of these cases are!"

I lowered my eyes. What happened to the old days when Mom was excited just to be home with me and Eddie?

My heart started to pound really hard. I think it was trying to tell me it was time to give Mom a clue about Eddie. The pounding moved up to my throat. I shook my head. I couldn't do it.

"Honey, what's wrong?" Mom asked. The air around her seemed to vibrate with memories of the hugs she used to give me when I was little and skinned my knees. The loving tone in her voice said, *Mommy's here. Everything will be all right.*

Part of me wanted to believe that she could kiss away all the hurts. But another part knew she'd fallen out of touch with our family months ago.

To keep from crying, I focused on the painting over the fake fireplace in the conference room. It was a gray picture of a foggy lake with a big black boulder in front. A few forlorn trees stood in the background. I'd never really looked at that painting before. Now I wondered why a law office would keep such a depressing picture in a place where clients came in with all their problems.

"That's a weird picture," I said.

"One of the partners knows the artist," said Mom. "Asa, you didn't answer my question. Is something wrong? Trouble at school?"

I shook my head. My pulse speeded up. If Mom kept guessing, she'd figure it out eventually.

"Are you fighting with Joy and Claire?"

I shook my head again.

"Is it Eddie?" Mom asked gently.

The muscles in my back tightened. Just hearing his name made my head throb. I stared at my soda so Mom wouldn't see the answer in my eyes. Eddie and I had deals. We had an understanding: don't upset Mom.

"Asa." Mom's voice sounded scared. Her eyes looked wide and panicky. "Please tell me he didn't hit you. Or...anything else."

The words struck me like a blast of cold water. How could she get things so wrong? I frowned. "No. Of course not."

Mom deflated into her seat. "Thank heavens," she murmured to herself. A second later she sat up again, her eyes flashing. "Is he drumming for Simon after I told him not to?"

"He...kind of found a loophole," I said slowly. My heart thudded against my chestbone. I hoped Eddie would forgive me. I swallowed hard. "The guy he's playing with isn't Simon. His name is...I can't remember, but he has frizzy hair."

Mom drummed her fingers on the table and thought about that for a minute. "Well," she said finally. "At least he isn't drinking."

I snorted to myself. How could she miss that? She'd been eager enough to check *my* breath the time I skipped school.

"Asa," Mom said, frowning suspiciously. "Is he drinking?"

"Not all the time," I said, real fast. "And I think maybe he quit."

"When was he drinking?" Mom demanded.

I squinted in disbelief. Was she really so busy with research and all her cases at work that she honestly didn't notice? Impossible.

I gave her the benefit of the doubt. "Maybe you still have a head cold and your nose isn't working right," I said.

Mom grabbed my arms. "Asa, how often have you smelled alcohol?"

Her grip tightened, scaring me. I pulled away.

"Only once," I blurted. That was a lie, but I'd already done enough damage.

Mom clenched her fists. "I can't believe this is happening all over again." She slammed her fists on the table. "I won't have it!"

My head spun. What was I thinking? I never should have told her! Alcohol was the reason she'd divorced my real dad. What if she divorced Eddie too?

I felt like I was falling into the middle of the earth where all that molten stuff is. Eddie was the closest thing I ever had to a dad. Even if he bugged me sometimes, I still wanted to keep him around.

Mom took a deep breath. "Asa, sweetie, I'm so sorry. I didn't mean to yell. I told myself I wasn't going to let it get to me if it happened." She took another breath, but this time it was a weird gasping noise that sounded like somebody trying not to cry. That's when I noticed her eyes were shiny.

Seeing her so close to tears sent a shudder through me. Mom was supposed to be the strong one. She was supposed to fix things. But what if that meant us leaving Eddie?

"Please don't hate him," I said, fighting my own tears.

"Oh, Asa," Mom said. She reached over and pulled me onto her lap. She held me in her arms and rocked gently. "I don't hate Eddie," she said in a soft voice. "He has a disease. That's why I've been going to Al-Anon, to help me understand it better."

"No!" I shouted, scrambling back to my own chair. "You're only going to Al-Anon 'cause Grandpa's an alcoholic. And my real dad. But not Eddie. Eddie's just…Eddie."

Mom leaned over and smoothed my hair. "Eddie has been an alcoholic in recovery for about seven years," she said. "Something made him slip. Maybe it was losing the orchestra, or maybe it was all that time alone when I had to work late. Maybe he just belongs back in AA." Mom sighed. "I wish you'd told me about this sooner, honey." She gave me another hug, then stood up. "I can't come home with you right now, but I promise to be there at five. If Eddie's drinking when you get home, just go next door to the Webers' until you see my car in the drive. All right?"

I nodded, feeling dazed. A cold shiver rolled down my back as I wobbled to my feet. I guess a part of me always knew Eddie was an alcoholic. The shiver subsided and left an aching lump in my throat. *Eddie is an alcoholic.* The ache started to throb. Tears tingled behind my eyes. I didn't want Mom to see.

"Gotta go, Mom," I said quickly, and tore out of the room.

Outside, I jammed my bike helmet over my head, swiped the water out of my eyes, and kicked off. I sniffled the whole way home. A normal dad, that's all I wanted.

Chapter Eighteen

Most of my tears had dried up by the time I coasted my bike down my street. Sometimes a good cry made me feel better. This time it had just left me feeling drained and headachy. I didn't even know if I'd have the energy for my date with Domino tonight. Right now all I wanted to do was lock myself in my room and duck my head under the pillow.

I stared down at the pavement as I rolled into my drive-way. I didn't even look up when I heard the *whacka-whacka* of a basketball bouncing on our drive. My ears tuned into another sound. Live electric guitar music, twanging and shrieking from the basement window. Eddie was practicing to a heavy metal CD. Just knowing he was home made my pulse whump nervously in my ears. What would it be like facing Eddie now that I knew the truth?

"Hey, Ace!"

I jumped, startled. Jason was usually the one practicing basketball. But this time it was Dom. He turned toward me without watching his last throw. The ball bounced off the backboard and rolled into the grass. Dom strode up to me. "Still coming over at tonight?" he asked.

An uneasy ripple surged through me. I wasn't sure if I wanted to see anybody tonight. I wasn't even sure if I could.

"Mom's staying home tonight," I said. "She might not let me come since I'm still grounded. Technically."

Dom's eyes were mischievous. "You mean your mom is cutting school? You should ground *her.*"

I wanted to laugh, but Eddie's guitar music stopped me. Would Eddie hate me when he found out I'd told Mom about his drinking? Would Mom yell at him when she got home? Would he leave us?

Dom thumped me in the arm. "Ace? You okay?"

How could I be okay? My family might be about to fall apart. I wasn't ready to tell Dom the whole truth, but I could tell a little of it. I took a deep breath and said, "I just found out Eddie has a disease. Don't tell anybody, okay?"

"What?" Dom looked shocked. "But he seems so healthy. It isn't cancer, is it?" he added in a horrified whisper. "Is Eddie going to die?"

I shook my head. "It's nothing like that," I said, rubbing my nose to hold off the tears.

"Good!" Dom said, sounding relieved. "I don't want anybody to die. Remember last winter when my granddad had that heart attack? For a whole week we didn't know if he was going to make it. That was the worst time of my life."

I remembered how quiet Dom had been at the bus stop that week. He hadn't wanted to talk about it until his grandfather was safely home from the hospital.

But there was a big difference between the ways people looked at heart disease and alcohol disease. Everybody still liked Dom's grandfather when he got sick. There were times when my mom hadn't acted very loving toward my grandfather when he had his disease. Now Eddie had it. I felt wobbly inside.

"I guess…" I took a deep breath. "I guess you have to still love people when they have diseases."

"Ace," Dom said. "You love them *more* when they're sick."

"Guess so," I said. Love sure was complicated.

Even Eddie's guitar music sounded complicated right now.

"I have to go," I said. "I'm still supposed to be grounded."

"Try to come over tonight if you can," Dom said.

I nodded, and headed toward my door.

"Ace," Dom called in a stage whisper.

I looked back.

"Tell Eddie you love him."

My insides jumped. "What?" I squeaked.

"He's sick, right?" Dom said with a shrug. "It'll make him feel better. It worked for my granddad."

My head filled with more questions as I shuffled inside my house. Could love stop Eddie's disease from giving him Russian roulette days like my grandpa had? Or could something as simple as telling him *I love you* turn him into a raging monster?

Eddie's energetic guitar music made it hard to believe he was sick. He sounded like he was having a total blast in the basement.

Did I love him? Even if I did, could I tell him? I didn't think I was brave enough for that. What if he laughed in my face?

In an instant I came up with a plan. I pulled my pony farm story out of my pack and sneaked down the hall to Eddie's study. I hid the story under the pile of test booklets on his desk. When Eddie found it, maybe he'd read between the lines like Mr. Evington had.

It was worth a chance. Eddie was worth a chance.

I was halfway out the study door when the phone rang. I rushed back to Eddie's desk and picked up the violin phone.

"Hello?"

"Is this Ed Clegg's place?" said a voice on the other end.

"Maybe." Mom always said not to give too much information to strangers over the phone.

"Close enough," the guy said. "Write this down for your dad: 'Vic Kelso called. There's been a cancellation. The audition's at seven now.' Got that?"

I scribbled the message on Eddie's message pad. "Got it," I said into the phone.

It wasn't till after the man had hung up that I realized he'd called Eddie my dad. First Mom, now strangers. I tried to say the word "dad" out loud but all I could manage was "duh."

It seemed easier to not call Eddie anything.

I ripped off the page with my note and carried it downstairs.

Eddie was playing with his eyes shut. I stood in front of him for a whole minute before he snapped out of his music trance and blinked at me. He grinned. "There she is!"

"Hi," I shouted over the music. "Phone message." I held it out.

Eddie stopped playing and turned off the stereo with the remote.

He skimmed my note in half a second. "Ho! That's what we like to see," he said in a jolly voice.

"We do?" I asked, not so sure.

"Oh yeah," Eddie said, eyes glistening. He put his guitar in its case and snapped the latches shut. "Even your mom will like this one. No playing in bars. Just anniversaries and class reunions, and an ongoing gig at the Holiday Inn outside

Ram's Head every Thursday night. The pay's even better than community orchestra. Now your mom won't have to work all those extra hours. See?" Eddie spread out his arms and grinned. "It's perfect."

I nodded, wanting to believe it was. "So you told Mom about it?" I asked quietly.

Eddie's smile disappeared. "Oh. Well. Not quite. I wanted to wait till after the audition tonight. I didn't want to get her hopes up in case I don't get the gig."

"Tonight?" I cried out. "You can't go tonight. Mom's coming home."

Eddie raised his eyebrows. "Why?"

"Because—because she misses us," I blurted in desperation. "She wants to have dinner with us and hang out."

Eddie hissed one of those words you say when you step in something a dog left on the sidewalk. He started to pace back and forth in front of Mom's drums.

"Two months," Eddie muttered. "She's perfectly content for two months, now all of a sudden she misses us?" He stopped pacing and spun toward me. "Why tonight? Can't she wait till tomorrow to miss us?"

My heart boomed to a guilty beat. Mom was coming home tonight because of what I, Asa Philips, had told her. I stared at my feet, hoping my hot face wasn't turning red.

"Asa," Eddie said in a low voice. "What's going on?"

Tears tingled at the back of my eyes. I clenched my fists, refusing to cry.

"Hey, wait a minute. You didn't tell your mother, did you?" he demanded.

"Mom figured it out on her own," I snapped. "She's not stupid."

"I never said she was."

"We can't lie to her anymore," I yelled. "We just—*can't!*"

My brain wasn't big enough to hold all our made-up stories anymore. Angry and confused tears flooded down my cheeks. I shuddered and sobbed into my hands. Then Eddie was at my side. He put his arm around my shoulders and guided me to the basement couch. I sat next to him, blubbering and gulping for air. Eddie didn't get nervous and ask me to stop the way he'd done the last time I cried in front of him. He didn't even ask if he could write a song about it. He just held me.

Gradually all the tears ran out. I sniffed and swiped at my wet face with the back of my hand.

"I, uh...I'm sorry, Ace," Eddie said in a gentle voice. "There's probably something uplifting and parental I'm supposed to say, but I don't have a clue what that is."

I sniffed again. What I wanted to hear were promises. Promises that he'd never lie again or ask me to lie. Promises that he'd never drink again. My head was throbbing. *But what good are promises?* I thought. *A person can't promise not to have a disease.* A new thought gave me an even bigger headache. *What if I had to be honest with him first?*

Deep down a part of me said, *Tell him and get it over with.*

My brain argued with itself for a few seconds. Finally, I sucked in some air and said in one breath, "Mom said you have a disease." I cringed on the inside, afraid of the truth. Afraid to look at Eddie in case those words made him mad.

"Maybe she's wrong," I added, real fast. "She's probably wrong. Mom still has booze phobia from Grandpa."

Eddie didn't answer.

My heart beat harder. If Eddie wanted to deny everything, to say it had all been a big mistake, this was his chance. Part of me almost hoped he would.

"Ace," he said finally.

Reluctantly I faced him. His eyes didn't look angry or ready to lie. They just looked sad.

"She's right," Eddie said, barely above a whisper.

I looked away again. When Eddie was quiet like this I could tell he was being honest with me. I stared into my lap. I didn't want any more lies between us. "I...uh...I put water in your flask."

I shut my eyes and cringed, waiting for Eddie to explode the way he had at the jazz band.

About ten long, silent seconds went by. I peered up at him from under my bangs. Eddie was looking back at me, but he wasn't giving me a death-ray stare. He didn't clench his teeth or anything. He just blinked at me.

"I know," he said softly. "I found that out two weeks ago."

I stared back in disbelief. "Did you hate me?"

"I wanted to wring your neck," he said, half teasing, half serious. "But since you weren't there at the time I had two other choices: either go out and buy another bottle or stop and think about...the whole drinking thing."

I hadn't smelled alcohol on Eddie in ages. Did that mean he'd given it up? My tensed muscles relaxed a tiny bit.

"Then it's okay for me to tell you that I emptied the bottle we hid in my closet and put water in there, too?" I asked.

"Geez, Asa," Eddie said. "That stuff isn't cheap."

"But you quit. You just said you quit!" I said.

"I said I'm thinking about it," Eddie huffed.

I sank deeper into the couch.

He let out a big sigh. "Look, Ace, I know you mean well," he said, tousling my hair. "But you can't help me like that, okay? I have to stop because I want to, not because somebody else wants it. And it's pretty tough."

I bowed my head. Then how *could* I help?

I took a deep breath. "Someone told me that people with diseases need extra love to help them get better," I said. "Do you think that works for any disease?"

"Oh Ace, I hope so," Eddie said, sounding tired. He stood up slowly, like he was worn out. "You have homework, don't you?" he said. "I'll start dinner."

I nodded.

Eddie's music had sounded so happy earlier. Now he plodded toward the staircase, looking depressed. There had to be some way to bring back his energy. Before he reached the bottom step I said, "Um?" to get his attention.

Eddie looked back.

"What about your audition tonight?" I asked.

Eddie frowned at the floor. "I don't know."

"I think you should tell Mom and go for it."

"I think you should do your homework," he said, and trudged up the stairs.

To show Eddie he was allowed to act like a dad today, I puffed out a sigh and thumped up the steps behind him.

In my room I actually did a few math word problems. It almost felt like a normal day doing homework. I barely even thought about my possible date with Domino. It didn't seem so important anymore. Then I heard Mom's car pull into our drive.

The sound revved my pulse into a nervous spin. I sprinted to my door and eased it open. I stuck my head into the hallway and listened. Then I heard the door from the garage open. Next, I heard Mom's shoes click across the tile floor in the dining area. I held my breath and waited for the yelling to start.

Nothing.

I let myself breathe again.

A few seconds later I heard Mom head down the hall. I ducked back into my room and gently closed the door. I pressed my ear against the wood. All I heard was the sound of water pattering in the master bedroom shower.

There are two kinds of quiet: the kind that feels cozy, and the kind that feels like a damp house with a leak in it. At supper we had the leaky kind.

Nobody talked much at the table. Eddie acted polite to Mom in a chilly way. Mom spoke in a quiet voice, but I sensed the volcano rumbling underneath.

This was our first tense meal since last summer and I wasn't sure I could handle it. Sitting there waiting for a big fight to explode any minute gave me nervous stomach cramps. On top of that, Eddie had fixed tacos, Spanish rice, and refried beans. Spicy foods were the last things my stomach needed.

I took one bite of rice, then pushed the rest around my plate to make it look like I'd eaten something. The sooner I could ask to be excused, the better. I had to get away, maybe even leave the whole house. "Um," I said, trying to sound casual. "Domino invited me over to his place to do homework. Can I go?"

"Sure," said Eddie.

I looked up in surprise. Mom always gave me permission to do stuff.

"Oh?" Mom said. "Are you making all the decisions about Asa now?"

Eddie frowned. "She asked me a question. I answered it."

"She didn't ask you specifically."

Eddie turned toward me. "Asa, tell Mom what 'um' means."

I started to say it didn't mean anything, but in a flash I understood. I had never realized it before, but *Um* was my name for Eddie. It was the perfect compromise if I couldn't call him Eddie or Dad to his face. That meant Eddie knew I was afraid of the name Dad. Knowing he knew made me blush.

Mom didn't seem to notice how big this moment was. We were teetering near an important step: the kid and the almost dad, searching for a name.

"Here's the thing," Mom said in her know-it-all voice. She sounded like Joy. "You can't just tell Asa it's okay to leave. I came home so we could be together as a family tonight."

"No, *here's* the thing," Eddie shot back. "You didn't bother to call and ask if your family had other plans tonight."

Mom's eyes flashed.

The two grains of rice I'd eaten collided from opposite ends of my stomach.

"Edward, are you telling me you have somewhere to go tonight?" asked Mom.

I held my breath. The fight was coming.

Eddie glared at his plate. He shoveled a forkful of refried beans into his mouth so he wouldn't have to talk.

"Well?" said Mom. "Do you?"

"Just tell her," I whispered to Eddie.

"Asa knows?" Mom shrieked. "You can tell *her,* but you can't tell me?" Her voice went from sounding angry to tearful. "Why won't you talk to me, Eddie?"

"You're too busy to hear anything I have to say." Eddie spoke so softly it was almost a whisper. "You're either studying all the time or too tired to talk." Now he sounded hurt.

"I'm listening now, honey," Mom said in a choked voice. "Talk to me now."

Of course he didn't. Even Mom had to know that wasn't how you got Eddie to open up. He needed quiet for a few seconds to collect his thoughts. Nobody could order Eddie to speak. He talked when he was ready.

Maybe he would have said something, but Mom didn't give him the chance. She pushed back her chair and flew down the hall.

I knew she was going to their bedroom to cry. My heart hammered at my ribcage.

Eddie put down his fork and sighed. "Guess I'd better go talk to her," he mumbled to himself and stood.

"Please don't yell at her," I whispered.

Eddie patted me on the shoulder. "Do the dishes, okay?" he said.

He disappeared down the hall, too.

I sat alone for half a second, then popped out of my chair. I dashed from the table to the kitchen and back again. I cleared and rinsed and stacked. Even though my whole body felt shaky, I didn't drop any glasses or dishes. The whole time I was cleaning up, I strained my ears to listen.

No voices yelled from their room. Nobody threw anything against the wall. Maybe they were making up, or maybe they were talking about divorce. *Please, not another divorce.* My head hurt.

I turned on the dishwasher and wiped down the counters.

Chapter Eighteen

According to the wall clock I had twenty minutes before my date with Dom. I scurried down the hall to the main bathroom for a quick shower, just in case.

No noise came from Mom and Eddie's room. I raced to my room and shakily tugged on a pair of torn jeans. I had to get out of there. If they were breaking up, I didn't want to know. I grabbed Eddie's blue dress shirt that I'd hung in my closet. I fumbled with the buttons. Still no sound. I jammed my feet into my Silhouettes.

"I'm studying at Domino's," I called toward their closed door.

"Okay," they said at the same time.

I froze. Wait a minute. They'd said it at the same time. Did that mean everything was okay between them again? There was no way to know.

Chapter Nineteen

Domino had told me to come over at seven-fifteen, but I couldn't wait that long. As soon as I heard his parents' car pull out of the drive I darted across the lawn to his back door.

Dom answered my knock. He wore gray sweatpants and a huge red plaid flannel shirt. It looked baggier on him than Eddie's shirt looked on me. "So what were you doing?" he asked. "Watching through the window to see when they left?"

"Couldn't wait to see that new video game," I lied.

"Hope you won't be too disappointed."

He led the way to the basement, which was set up like a den. It had wall-to-wall carpeting, a comfy brown couch, and matching chairs that faced a wide-screen TV.

"Do your parents fight much?" I asked as Dom popped in the game cartridge.

He snorted. "Are you kidding? I thought they'd never leave tonight. First Mom comes out in this ugly green dress and says to Dad, 'Does this make me look fat?'" In a deep voice Dom answered for his dad. "'You always look fat, dear.'" He rolled his eyes. "That's my dad's idea of a joke. Then Mom tells him his necktie makes him look pasty. So he changes it. Then Mom puts on another outfit, but it clashes with Dad's new tie so he has to find another one. It was crazy over here."

I knew Dom was making half the stuff up as he went, but his story made me laugh.

"You like that story?" Dom said with a shy grin. "Then you'll love this."

He handed me a game pad and took the other one for himself.

Domino's "new" video game turned out to be a kiddie game left over from a visit with one of his little cousins. The object was to steer a cartoon caterpillar through a maze and pick up letters of the alphabet. The first one to get all twenty-six in order won. It was so stupid it was funny. At least it took my mind off Mom and Eddie.

Dom and I bumped shoulders to make each other mess up. The shoulder bumping turned into leaning into each other. Sometime around the letter *R* we kissed. Just a quick kiss. It made me feel like a caterpillar was running a maze in my stomach.

"So..." Domino said. He looked away and I saw that his ears had turned red. "Wanna be my girlfriend or something?"

Just so he wouldn't think I was too eager, I waited for a quiet count of ten. Then I shrugged and said, "Okay. Sure."

Domino cracked up laughing. "This is awesome! I got a girlfriend before Jason! Wait here, I wrote you a poem."

I raised my eyebrows. Dom had written a *poem?* For me?

He hopped off the couch and tore up the steps. A minute later he bounced down next to me on the couch again. He opened a folded piece of notebook paper. "I worked on this when I was in detention. It even rhymes. Listen:

> *Who's the best card in the deck?*
> *Which card smiles and has a neck?*

> *Maybe it's the Asa Spades*
> *Whose hair's too short to wear in braids.*
> *Or maybe it's the Asa Hearts*
> *Who sometimes burps but never—"*

"Hold it!" I said. "Stop right there. Is this some kind of—"

"Wait," Domino said. "You have to hear all of it:

> *Could she be my Asa Clubs*
> *Who never writes with pencil nubs?*
> *Or Diamond Ace who smiles and all*
> *When I see her in the hall?*
> *I think my Asa's all of these.*
> *I love her better than Swiss cheese!"*

Dom looked up with a hopeful glow in his eyes. "Like it?"

It was the sweetest, dumbest poem I'd ever heard. It sounded like a little kid had written it. That was when it hit me: Domino was a kid. He was a kid with parents who acted like grown-ups, even when they teased each other about their clothes. I envied Dom so much it hurt.

"Well?" he said, still smiling.

An instant later I knew I loved Domino back. To prove it I socked him in the arm. "Good poem, boyfriend."

He looked serious. "To make it official you have to sit with me on the bus."

I nodded. Claire wouldn't mind. I hoped.

"But not all the time," he added. "And don't call me up too many times at night or it'll give Jason something to give me a hard time about."

"Okay, but don't make any more rules or it'll take the fun out of it."

"Just one more." Domino put his arm around my shoulders. "I get to do this."

I snuggled against him, feeling fluttery in the stomach, but cozy too. He leaned over and kissed my cheek. I turned my head toward him. We touched lips. The next thing I knew we were tangled up on the couch, kissing and breathing all heavy. The world disappeared.

The sudden trill from the upstairs phone sent us crashing back to earth.

Domino sat up so fast I fell off the couch.

"I gotta get that," he said, and sprinted up the steps.

I sat up, panting for breath.

A second later Dom called down, "Ace, it's your mom."

My legs turned to rubber. What if Mom was calling to say we were leaving Eddie? I stumbled up the steps to Dom's kitchen phone.

Dom held out the receiver.

I covered the mouthpiece. "How'd she sound?" I whispered.

Dom shrugged. "Like your mom."

"Hello?" I said. I swallowed hard to get the big lump of fear out of my throat.

"Sweetie, you need to come home now. We're going out."

I slumped against Dom's fridge in relief. If they were going out together that had to mean they made up.

"Can't I stay here while you're out?"

"No, honey, I meant the whole family's going together."

Mom mentioned something about Eddie's audition. It was hard concentrating with Domino standing behind me, tickling my sides. I nudged him away with my elbow and tried not to laugh into the phone.

Even though I pleaded with her, Mom didn't give in. She wanted me to come straight home. Eddie was already in the car, warming up the engine.

I sighed and hung up. "I have to go. We're having some kind of family night."

Dom made a face. "Well," he said, cheering up again, "At least you can sit with me on the bus tomorrow."

I grinned. "Can't wait," I said.

We only had time for one more quick kiss, but it was enough to wrap me in a warm glow all the way to Eddie's car. I settled into the back seat, still feeling cozy.

"Sweetie, didn't you wear a coat when you went over there?" Mom asked from the front seat.

I didn't feel cold at all. Especially when I noticed that the tension between Mom and Eddie was gone. Whatever they'd said to each other must have worked.

Mom asked Eddie to turn on the heat. In a few minutes warm air rolled over me.

Eddie's audition was at a music shop in Elsmore, a little town north of Ram's Head. In the parking lot beside Kelso's Music, Eddie pulled his guitar case out of the trunk. Mom gave him a kiss for good luck.

He carried his guitar case through the store to the studio in the back. Mom and I stayed up front and browsed around the guitars and wind instruments. We didn't want to make him nervous.

"I wish he still had the orchestra," Mom said softly. "He was so happy then. And they performed in an auditorium."

I nodded. What she meant was, a place with no booze.

We passed through an open doorway into a room filled with nothing but drums and drum accessories. Mom's eyes lit up. "Look at the cymbals!"

There were dozens of them on stands and hanging on the wall. Mom rushed toward one on a stand. It was called a ping ride cymbal. It actually made a loud *ping* when she flicked it. She smiled at the sound.

"So this is what Eddie and I decided," Mom said suddenly. She took a big breath. "Family comes first. Whether Eddie gets this gig or not, I'm cutting my hours at work."

I nodded, liking their decision already.

"The other thing is, for this family to work, each of us needs to be in a program." She lowered her voice even though nobody else was around. "I've got Al-Anon, Eddie's going to start going to AA again, and we'd like you to go to Alateen."

My smile disappeared. The family plan was supposed to mean more homemade cookies around the house and a mom and dad to tell me good night every night. Maybe Mom needed Al-Anon and Eddie needed Alcoholics Anonymous. But why did I need help?

"I'm okay, Mom," I said. "I told you before I don't need that."

Mom rested her hand under my chin and tilted my head toward her. "Guess what, sweet cakes? You *do* need it. Eddie needs our love and support. Alateen will teach you how give him the right kind of help." She raised an eyebrow. "For one thing, you can't hide alcohol for him."

I gasped. "Who told you I hid alcohol?"

She thumped me lightly under the chin. "Who do you think? He also told me about that excuse he wrote for you. You guys really had a time for yourselves, didn't you?" Mom said, but she didn't sound angry about it. She put her arm around me. "It's going to be okay, kiddo. You'll like Alateen."

I hated it already.

A second later Mom discovered a double bass drum set with sparkling blue shells. She zipped across the room and bounced onto the drum throne. Before I realized what was happening, she pulled a pair of drumsticks out of her purse and started playing! Okay, so it sounded like she knew what she was doing, smashing cymbals and rumbling over the toms while her feet danced over the two bass drum pedals. But I still backed out of the room. Normal kids don't have moms who play drums in public like that.

I wanted to check on Eddie anyway. I walked back the way I'd seen him go. I scooted down a narrow hallway with empty practice rooms on both sides. A sign at the end of the hall said "Studio," with an arrow pointing the way. A few seconds later I found the control booth and eased inside.

It was dark except for a tiny lamp near a bunch of knobs and switches. Brighter light shone from a big glass window above the controls. Eddie and his guitar were on the other side of the glass. So were three other musicians. Eddie looked like a kid compared to the other members of the band. There was a guy with a huge belly at the keyboards, a balding guy on bass guitar, and a skinny, gray-haired guy on drums. At the moment they were all laughing.

"You lost?" a voice asked from behind me.

I peered over my shoulder.

A tall man with dark brown skin had just come in, carrying a Styrofoam cup.

"I uh, know the guy who's auditioning," I said.

He flashed a smile. "Well then, pull up a stool." He shook my hand. "Ty Morris, sound tech. You must be a little Clegg."

I was actually a little Philips, but I just nodded and said, "I'm Asa."

A second later the band started up. Music came through a speaker in the booth. It sounded like an old rock ballad, maybe from the fifties. Eddie looked relaxed and confident and that was exactly how his guitar sounded.

"He's good," I said.

"You know it," Ty agreed.

I smiled, relieved. Now that I knew Eddie was okay, I slid off the stool. "Thanks," I said and slipped out.

As soon as I reached the main showroom Mom hustled up to me. "Where'd you go?"

"I wanted to see the audition," I said with a shrug.

"How's it going?"

I laughed out loud. "Better than ever!"

Mom let out a big, relieved sigh. She smiled and gave me a hug.

A little while later, Eddie ambled into view, carrying his case. He gave Mom a nod and walked out the door. Mom and I scurried after him. He didn't say a word while he unlocked the trunk and put his guitar case inside.

"Eddie, come on," Mom said. "The suspense is killing us."

He closed the trunk and faced Mom. His grin was so wide, even weather satellites flying overhead had to know he got the job. He opened his arms and Mom practically jumped into them. They hugged real tight and started to kiss. Right in the middle of the parking lot with lights shining on them and everything.

"Hey!" I said. "Don't embarrass me out here."

Eddie laughed and pulled me into a group hug.

We decided to celebrate with hot fudge sundaes at Friendly's. Before we ordered, Eddie gave more details about the band. They rehearsed on Wednesday nights from eight to ten and played at the Holiday Inn Thursdays, ten to midnight. Two weekends a month they'd have anniversaries and reunions and stuff in the afternoons.

Then Mom had to ruin the festive mood by leaning against Eddie and saying, "I told Asa about our programs."

Eddie nodded and shook a packet of sugar into his iced tea.

Mom smiled across the booth at me. "After you left my office today I made a few calls." She pulled a piece of notepaper from her purse. "There's an Alateen meeting tomorrow afternoon. I thought I'd take you to school and then pick you up after—"

"Not tomorrow!" I said quickly. "I have to ride the bus tomorrow." I didn't tell her about my promise to Domino. I just told her it was a matter of life and death.

Mom raised an eyebrow at me, then went back to her paper. "Okay, there's another one on Saturday afternoon."

I shook my head again. "I'm working on a project with Joy."

Mom huffed. She checked the schedule again. "All right, we have one more. Monday night. Eddie, you'll have to take her to that one. My meeting's half an hour earlier at a different church. And, as luck would have it, there's an AA meeting same time, same place."

"Oh goodie," Eddie said, half joking, half sarcastic.

The waiter showed up with our ice cream. We stopped talking till he left. Then I leaned across the table and whispered to Mom, "Can't I start going next month or something?"

"Give it up, Ace," Eddie teased. "When Mom gets an idea she doesn't let go."

I frowned and dipped my spoon into my hot fudge. It was only Tuesday. Maybe things would get real busy at the law office between now and then and Mom would forget all about Alateen.

Chapter Twenty

Nobody mentioned Alateen the whole rest of the week. I hoped that meant they really had forgotten. At dinner on Monday I said to Mom, "Hey, after I do the dishes I'm going over to—"

"No," Eddie cut in.

I turned toward Eddie. "But we have this science take-home test," I explained. "Dom and I aren't in the same class but we have the same teacher so we thought—"

"No," Eddie said again.

"Mom," I pleaded.

"You know what day this is," she said. "You've got some-place to go tonight."

"Can't I go next week?" I asked. "This is a test. We won't be messing around, we'll be working."

"You can work on it over the phone before you leave," Mom said.

"This isn't fair," I muttered.

After dinner Mom left for Al-Anon. I slouched on the stool at the snack bar and dialed Dom's number from the kitchen phone. I hoped when Eddie saw me actually doing homework he'd go to his AA meeting by himself and let me stay here.

"Mom wants me to do family stuff again," I told Domino

over the phone. "We have to do the test over the phone. She won't let me come over."

"That's okay," Domino said in a cheerful voice. "Hold on while I get my science book."

I spread my notes over the snack bar. The test was mostly multiple choice and true and false. It was still hard, especially when we got to the geology part with the igneous and sedimentary rock questions. I had kind of skipped that chapter when it was assigned because it was so boring.

"The answer to eleven is C," Domino announced while I flipped to the rock chapter.

"You sure?" I asked, still hunting for the right page.

"Has to be. Look at the choices."

Before I could read them, Eddie showed up in a coat and black felt cap. He carried a bottle of vodka under his arm. He stepped up to the sink and opened the bottle.

"A and B are obviously joke answers," Domino was saying over the phone. "It can't be D because that was the answer to ten and Gold would never put two Ds in a row."

Eddie took off his cap and held it over his heart with one hand. With his other hand he poured the vodka down the drain.

"Ace? You still there?" asked Domino.

"Uh huh," I said, watching Eddie. I wondered if that was the watered-down bottle I had hidden in my closet or if it was another one.

"Twelve is true."

Eddie set the emptied bottle on the counter by the sink. "Time to go," he said, without turning around. "Hang up now."

"Did you read the question?" I said into the phone.

"You don't have to read it," said Domino. "True and false questions are always true. That way Mr. Gold reinforces the right answers."

"Unless he wants us to recognize wrong ones. Hold on while I read this thing."

"Hang *up*, Asa," Eddie said from the sink.

I frowned at the distraction then skimmed the question a second time. "No, I think it's false."

Eddie turned around now and took the phone right out of my hand.

"Domino, you'll have to excuse Asa," he said into the mouthpiece, "she has to go somewhere now."

Then he hung up on my boyfriend!

"You can't do that!" I cried.

"Get your shoes and coat."

I squinted at him.

"We're leaving in one minute," he said.

"I can't. I'm doing homework."

"Shoes and coat," he repeated. "Fifty-seven seconds."

"I have to change my clothes at least," I said.

Eddie was all showered and shaved and wearing cords and a decent shirt.

"No time. Shoes and coat," he said in a stern voice. "In forty seconds you'll be dragged out by force."

I made one of those huffing sounds to let him know I didn't like being ordered around. Then I stomped to my room. Out of curiosity I checked the back of my closet. No bottle. Now I knew what he'd just poured down the drain.

"I'm coming back there in ten, nine, eight..."

"All right!" I screamed at him. I scuffed my feet into my sneakers but didn't tie them. Out of protest I didn't zip my jacket either. On the way to the car a frigid blast of late-October air hit me. I pretended not to notice.

Eddie didn't say anything. He put the car in reverse and backed out of the driveway. Neither of us spoke on the short drive to town.

Mom had told me kids just talked at Alateen meetings. I shivered and hugged my arms. What did they talk about? Would they make me say stuff? On top of that, I wouldn't know anybody. Who would I sit with?

Eddie pulled into the Presbyterian Church parking lot in the center of town. He locked the car doors and pushed through the wind to the red front doors. I scurried after him.

Inside Eddie rested a hand on my shoulder and walked me down the hall. It felt like we were on the way to my execution. Just outside the door to one of the Sunday school classrooms he turned toward me and said, "Looks like this is where your group is meeting. I'll be upstairs."

"But—"

"We'll meet at the car at eight-thirty, right? Right," he said then turned away before I could argue.

I watched him walk quickly down the hall with his hands in his pockets. After he disappeared around the corner I peeked inside the classroom. Half a dozen kids stood around, talking and laughing. More kids came in. I inched through the door behind them. I wanted to stay invisible long enough to find out what this was all about. Maybe Eddie got the room wrong. Maybe this was choir practice. If it was, I'd stay and sing. I'd even do Bible study. I didn't want to go to Alateen.

I turned toward the door just as Jennifer Terrell walked inside. I gaped at her. The second she saw me she did a double take.

"What are you doing here?" we said at the same time.

Jennifer grabbed me and pulled me to an empty corner of the room.

"You can't tell *anybody* you saw me here," she said in a desperate whisper.

"You can't tell anybody about me either," I said, feeling just as desperate.

"Wait a minute." Jennifer frowned. "Are you here for Alateen?"

I wanted to tell Jennifer I had the wrong room. I wanted to tell her I was really just looking for choir practice. But in the end, I nodded.

"Is this your first time?" she asked.

I stared at the floor.

"Asa, I'm sorry," Jennifer said in a quiet voice. "I didn't know anyone in your family had a drinking problem."

My head snapped up. I frowned at her, insulted.

"I know it's not easy. I hated coming here at first," Jennifer said. "But I kept coming back because of my grandmother. She's an alcoholic."

I was too shocked to reply. I'd never dreamed that someone as popular as Jennifer Terrell might have family problems.

"Come on," Jennifer said. "You can sit next to me."

I was still in a daze when she led me to one of the folding chairs set up in a semicircle in the middle of the room. I dropped into the chair beside her.

Jennifer nudged me. "You'll be okay," she whispered.

I nodded, but I wasn't so sure. Mom had said Alateen was anonymous. If I'd had any idea someone I knew would be here, I would have waited in the cold, dark parking lot until eight-thirty. I didn't want to tell the most popular girl in my grade about Eddie. In fact, I didn't want to tell *anybody* about Eddie.

"So you didn't wear the pink and red fad laces last Thursday," Jennifer said.

I folded my arms and stared into my lap, thinking about Thursday. Domino had to be at school early that day, so I sat with Claire. My Silhouettes and all the laces were jammed at the bottom of my pack, just waiting for the next fad day. When I spotted Rachel and Hilary at the bus stop wearing pink and red laces, I actually unzipped my pack and reached for them.

Then I stopped. I knew if I put on those shoes and laces somebody would invite me to Jennifer's table for lunch again. That meant I'd miss sitting with Claire and Joy. On top of that it was chocolate pudding day. Domino's friends always painted mustaches on themselves on chocolate pudding day. Jennifer's clique probably wouldn't appreciate that kind of humor. I stuffed the Silhouettes back into my pack.

I liked Dom's funny friends. I liked sitting with Claire and Joy so we could whoop and point and laugh at the crazy boys with chocolate pudding mustaches. I enjoyed giving Domino a hard time about his pudding goatee.

I didn't tell all that to Jennifer. I just shrugged and said, "Well, you know, the fad is kind of..." My voice trailed away.

"Yeah," Jennifer said with a sigh. "I know."

Before we could say any more, a wide lady in a blue tent dress came in. She looked like a choir director. She even had one of those jolly choir director voices when she asked everybody to have a seat. All the kids plopped into their chairs.

But it wasn't choir practice. It was Alateen. My nerves jangled as the meeting officially started. Everybody got quiet.

First the lady in charge handed a little card to the girl on her left. It had the Twelve Steps printed on it. The steps were originally made up for the people in Alcoholics Anonymous, but Alateen follows them too. They're things people try to do to make sense out of life when it gets messed up from alcohol.

We each took a turn reading a step. I got the tenth one, "Continued to take personal inventory and when we were wrong promptly admitted it."

I didn't hear Jennifer read Step Eleven. I was too busy wanting to promptly admit I didn't belong here. My life wasn't messed up from alcohol. Eddie never passed out from drinking or turned mean or threw things the way my other dad did back in the old days. Eddie had even dumped out the vodka bottle I used to hide for him. Wasn't that good enough? Couldn't I go home now?

Then I started to worry about Eddie. What if he was only pretending to go to his meeting to make Mom happy? What if he had driven away and forgotten all about me?

I shot out of my chair in a panic. I tore from the room and sprinted to the exit. I didn't let myself breathe again until I saw Eddie's Escort sitting in the parking lot right where he'd left it. Maybe he was upstairs after all.

I ducked back inside, but I was too embarrassed to go back to my own meeting. I headed upstairs where Eddie was supposed to be. I stopped to listen at the first closed door. That's when I heard, "My name's Edward and I'm an alcoholic."

My legs gave out when I recognized the voice. I slid all the way to the floor and listened from there.

"Hello, Edward," a bunch of people in the room said back.

Eddie told everyone a quick version of his life story. He talked about being a kid genius, but it wasn't Mom's version of the happy little boy who got to travel. He said he was under so much pressure to play well, he started drinking at age eleven. He had to quit touring two years later because half the time he was either too drunk or too hung over to practice.

He quit other jobs for the same reason. After he quit being Mr. Music on TV he stayed sober for almost seven years. That ended last Christmas when somebody at work gave him a bottle of vodka as a present.

"When the walls didn't cave in after that first drink," said Eddie, "I decided I was that one guy in a million who could go back and not get caught up in it. I was wrong."

Slowly I rose, feeling better already. That was Step Ten. He'd admitted he had a problem. Eddie was cured! Now that his troubles were solved, I headed back to my own meeting. I still didn't have the nerve to go back in, so I listened outside that door too.

Hardly anybody complained about his or her parents. One girl had a situation sort of like mine, a father who drank and an alcoholic stepfather. She said she hated the disease of alcoholism, but not the alcoholics in her life.

I almost said, "How do you do that?" out loud. The answer came when she repeated one of those slogans they seemed to use a lot: "One day at a time."

A boy said his mother was five months sober. Before he used to worry about her all the time, but now he was learning to change his attitude. "I think of her as having alcoholism in remission," he said. "She could relapse like with any disease, but I'm working at staying in the present. All I have is now."

Other kids mumbled in agreement.

Even Jennifer talked about her grandmother, who'd been living with the family since Jennifer was eight.

I can't remember everything everybody said. Some kids sounded angry but most of them sounded more positive. Just as the meeting began to close, I slipped back down the hall ahead of everybody else.

I met Eddie at the car.

We didn't talk all the way home. I was glad for the silence because I had a lot to think about. If Jennifer was brave enough to go to Alateen, maybe I should give it another try. If Mom made me go again, I'd stay in my chair.

Eddie's car rolled into our driveway. Mom's car was already in the garage. The motion sensor light above the back door blinked on. Eddie cut the engine.

"Wait," he said as I reached for the door handle. "Can we talk for a minute?"

I sat back in a slow, nervous kind of way. I stared out the windshield, into the dark. Did he know I'd spied on him at his AA meeting? All that stuff was supposed to be secret.

I waited.

If Eddie was going to lecture me, he sure was taking his time. He tapped his thumbs against the steering wheel.

"I read your story," Eddie said in a quiet voice.

I sank into my seat. I wanted to shrink into myself so it wouldn't hurt as much when he told me how stupid it was.

"I showed it to your mom too," he added. "We both liked the ending."

The light over the door blinked off. When my eyes adjusted to the darkness, I glanced over at Eddie. He was staring straight ahead. "We kind of talked and we decided you probably do need a father," Eddie said. He thumped the steering wheel again. "I'm not sure what kind of a dad you want."

My stomach quivered. "I don't know either," I said. But I did know. I was just afraid to put it into words. What if I told Eddie what I wanted and then found out he wasn't interested in the job?

"Whatever you're expecting," he said slowly, "it's a safe bet I won't measure up. The thing is, unless your other dad shows up to make some kind of claim, I'm it. Warts and all."

"You have warts too?" I asked. I didn't mean it to be funny, but Eddie chuckled.

"No. I meant..." Eddie puffed out his cheeks the way Mom does when she has bad news. "Man, this is hard."

"You hate me," I guessed.

"No, I don't," he said indignantly. "I'm not perfect, is what I meant. I really care about you, Asa, I'm just not very good at expressing it."

Now it was my turn to think things over. I breathed in some courage and said, "Am I supposed to call you Dad now?"

Eddie looked away. "Only if you want to."

"You want me to?"

"Hmmm. Let's see," he said. "Dad. Daaaad. Dah-dee." He tried saying it in several accents and funny voices. I couldn't help laughing.

"Yeah, okay," he said with a shrug. "Try it out."

I smiled and said, "Dad?" in a timid voice.

"WHAT?" he screamed. Then he grinned at me. "How was that?"

"Perfect," I said, laughing again. Then I said, "Um, Dad?"

"Um-Dad?" he teased. "That's two names."

I gave him a shove. "No, come on, I was asking something serious," I said. But I kept smiling. "Okay…um…Dad? I mean, *just* Dad."

"Spit it out, Ace, it's getting cold out here."

I inhaled, then said in one breath, "Are you done drinking forever?"

Eddie—I mean Dad—stopped smiling. He gripped the steering wheel with both hands and leaned back in his seat. "It's not that simple," he said in a soft voice. "Forever scares me. Even a week from now scares me. I hope I'll stay sober, but I've been through times in the past when all I could guarantee was one minute at a time."

That reminded me of the kid whose mother was in remission. I guess my new dad was too.

"It's okay," I whispered. "One minute is a good start."

Dad leaned over and kissed my cheek. "Thanks."

It was the least I could do. He'd given me a hundred ponies for my ninth birthday.

Many groups and organizations provide information and support to families and friends of alcoholics. For more information regarding Alateen, the organization mentioned in this book, please visit the Al-Anon Family Group's website at **www.al-anon.alateen.org.**